Her Men

Abe Levy

Her Men

Abe Levy

Those are people who died, died.
Those are people who died, died.
They were all my friends, and they died.

– Jim Carroll

HER END.

Nini reached out for his hand. Despite a nearly full moon, it was dark. When the fog rolls in, burying the Mendocino coast, it gets dark. Black. She took a couple of steps, and faint wisps of gray vapor began to swirl in her eyes. She couldn't be sure if it was the fog, somehow illuminated by random beams of light, lost in the night like the two of them, or just her drunken rods and cones doing their best to please her sleepy eyes.

"Where are you?"

She turned back and could barely make out his silhouette against the distant lights of the inn across the road. Waves crashed against the rocks behind her, nearly drowning out her voice, but he heard her.

"Here," he said.

She could hear his friendly smile in his voice, though she couldn't see his face. He caught up to her and as their hands finally met, they stepped off the road and onto the grassy trail that led to the small cottage they were staying in, just yards from the edge of the world...

It was a rocky edge, lined with eucalyptus and cypress, that jagged its way around three-quarters of the cottage, dropping 75 feet to the broken shore below.

He led her down the trail toward the cottage. He had done it many times without benefit of light, stumbling home from nights of partying at his mother's inn.

"I can't see you," she said, making a futile attempt to wave the gray wisps off. They persisted, and instead she grabbed his hand with both of hers now.

"We're almost there, careful … step up," he said, as he slowed the pace to climb a couple of steps that were carved into the earth.

She smiled, knowing he couldn't see her face. She had made her feelings very clear to him, but still shied from expressing them too obviously, too frequently, fearing that he would tire of her more easily that way, as so many had in the past. She didn't want to feel this way, though. She had a patient optimism that this was different, and perhaps it was. The cold air on her face cooled her cheeks, which began to flush in the invisible night air. She wanted to feel this night. Really feel it. Not just remember it, but have it seared into her, burned into her flesh, like a tattoo on the bloody side of her skin that only she could see from inside. That she would have forever.

"I should have left the lights on," he lamented.

"It's OK. I like the dark. With you. I want to give you something ..." Her voice softened. "… here in the dark."

She could hear his smile before he even spoke.

"Yeah? What?" He knew what, and knowing only made the anticipation that much sweeter.

"Head."

A soft laugh came from his black spot next to her. But she didn't take it the wrong way. She knew that he was kind and was not laughing at her, but rather at the notion of her giving him another blowjob so soon after the last, which she had given him in the bathroom of the inn, just a couple of hours before.

"You sure you don't want to go inside?"

She pulled him off the trail. She could smell the wet eucalyptus and cypress trees, and led him toward them, triangulating their smell with the sound of their leaves rustling in the wind.

She could feel the roots of the tree under her feet and reached out, touching its slick, wet bark. She pulled him around, leaning him against the tree. They kissed. It was a sweet kiss. They both knew what was about to happen, and neither felt the need to lean into it with heavy petting. The kiss lasted longer than either expected. There was no rush. It was a kiss like their first. Two people who had known each other for a long time, kissing because it was time and because they had always wanted to.

Finally, Nini stepped back. For a moment, he thought he saw her soft, round face, her blonde bangs cutting a straight line across her brow. But if he did, it didn't last, and once again he saw only black.

He waited in anticipation … but nothing happened. He laughed again. Still nothing.

"Nini?" he asked. Only the crash of the waves hitting the rocks far below echoed back at him. He reached out for her. Nothing. He nearly tripped over the exposed roots of the tree, then stepped forward into the blackness. Nothing. Nothing. Nothing. Seventy-five feet of nothing.

He hit the rocks only inches from Nini and bounced into the water. Her body had already slipped into the surf and was violently slamming into a sharp, black rock. His body tumbled in the eddy like a sock in a dryer, sometimes disappearing for a few seconds beneath the surface, but then rising again, as if it were fighting for a breath.

In the morning, as the sun slowly melted the thick fog back into the sea, both their battered, lifeless bodies floated side by side, each wave pushing them together, then apart, then together again.

MIGUEL.

Nini and I sat on the old wooden steps that led up to what passed for a videogame arcade on the second floor of the general store and the post office. It was one of only four large, non-residential buildings in town. Frogger, Donkey Kong and a foosball table were its only offerings, but it was the center for virtually all daytime teenage activity. Not that I was a teenager. Nini was, though. Just. At 13 she was bursting with teenage angst, sexuality and acne. Her breasts had recently ballooned in size to double Ds, and she was starting to get some attention for it. This pleased her, and she would often stand in front of the mirror in the bathroom, turning this way and that, trying to get a glimpse of what the boys must see when they looked at her. She knew she wasn't one of the prettiest girls at school, being short with bad skin, but now she had something they didn't. She had big tits. And she wasn't fat. She wasn't skinny, but she wasn't a fat girl. There were girls at school with tits as big as hers, but they were all big girls, fat girls, so it didn't count. Nini was a normal-sized girl — this was the '80s, and normal didn't yet mean rail thin. She sometimes verged on "plump," her waistline expanding and contracting as she hopped on and off her self-styled diets and exercise regimens. Bouts of serious acne plagued her, but even that really didn't matter anymore. She had big tits, and for guys that liked big tits, that was enough.

Miguel liked big tits. He was first-generation American, but while he spoke perfect English, he had a self-conscious Latin accent, softly rolling his "R"s, adding a sing-songy lilt to the ends of his sentences. Being Mexican might have been a problem for most guys looking to get some action from a white girl in a rural farming community, but Miguel had so much swagger, so much self-confidence and — most importantly — such fantastic timing, that it became an advantage.

Miguel had come along just as breakdancing fever swept through our tiny town. Myself, along with five or six other boys, had become obsessed, going so far as to name ourselves the "Tomales Beat Jammers" and feebly attempt to learn the simplest moves. Most of the girls in town — there weren't many — Nini included, had taken a more distant, barely attentive interest. They watched and teased as we lugged our square of green kitchen linoleum down the street to the old defunct gas station and attempted the back spin and the centipede. But this all changed when Miguel arrived.

He had moved from nearby Santa Rosa. Population 80,000, but it might as well have been the Bronx or L.A. He was the real deal. A real breakdancer from the city. Within a week of his arrival, Miguel was the president of the Tomales Beat Jammers. And suddenly we were cool. Every girl in town was hot for Miguel and was now a fan of our troop. They leaned against the walls of the old gas station, all in a row — there were only seven or eight girls in town once the daily migration to and from the high school from outlying areas was finished for the day — watching Miguel dance, instruct his acolytes and generally show off. He knew he was a big deal, and he knew just how to capitalize on it. He had surveyed the lay of the land and was now just waiting for the sheep to come to the wolf.

Nini's best friend, Meghan, made the first move, asking Miguel to play doubles Frogger with her. He graciously accepted, and as he and Meghan went up the stairs, Nini and I exchanged a vaguely annoyed glance, then got up and dutifully followed them up to the game room, which was crowded with parachute pants and red pleather Michael Jackson–jacket knockoffs.

Miguel draped himself over the game next to Meghan, smiling with his wide, toothy smile that was capped by a thin mustache, but his eyes were on Nini … or on Nini's tits, anyway. Miguel loved big tits. Meghan had small breasts but was prettier than Nini. She had always received more attention from boys than Nini, but that was beginning to change as it became clear that her cups had maxed out.

Nini pretended not to notice Miguel watching her. Meghan did, too, but it frustrated her and affected her game.

"Your turn, Miguel," Meghan said, dryly. As pretty as she was, she had a hard, sometimes sharp cadence that bordered on sarcasm which could put boys off, as much as they longed for her soft, blonde hair and trim, athletic body.

Miguel smiled again, his lips spreading out over his large, white teeth.

"Oh yeah, Meghan … . I'm gonna flip it, and flop it. Froggy-froggy …" Miguel purred from under his mustache, as he slid between Meghan and the joystick. While his preference was Nini's tits, he was no fool and knew that he could easily keep all his options open by feeding Meghan's kitty a nibble here and a nibble there. Besides, if he wanted to get in there without making the first move, which was clearly his M.O., he had to force Nini's hand.

His frog got run over by a truck. Meghan stepped back up to the joystick. Miguel wasn't any good at videogames, but it didn't matter. His suave, clichéd, Latin-lover play worked flawlessly on all of us. He was a god. Nini was still ignoring him. Even as the rest of us crowded around the game as we always did, Nini hung back, talking to Crow, a neighbor kid with red hair and perpetually bloodshot eyes from all the pot smoke that hung in the air at his mom's house. They were talking about the true nature of "light" cigarettes. He had just informed her that it wasn't "light" tobacco at all, but rather a ring of perforations around the filter, which allowed more air in.

"Oh my God, you're right!" she exclaimed, as she scrutinized a half-smoked butt from her pack of Marlboro lights.

Miguel stood behind Meghan as she expertly guided her frog across the freeway. Growing impatient, he slid one hand — the nearest to Nini — around Meghan and rested it on her joystick hand.

"That's it, easy … go with the flow … slow and easy …" Miguel said, slipping his "S"s to accentuate his accent. "Ssssslow and easssy." We knew lots of Hispanic kids, but none of them spoke like Miguel. He played it to the hilt.

Meghan couldn't take it. This was her game. It meant something to her. She had high score. She wasn't about to let Miguel's clumsy hand cost her the game.

"Miguel, get off! You're messing up my game!"

Miguel pulled back. He was in shock, not used to being dismissed in such a way. But he quickly came to his senses as Meghan shook him off and nimbly jumped her frog onto a turtle's back. He seized the moment, and in an inspired recovery, played the pain to the hilt. He actually let a tear fall from his eye. A spectacular, lone tear rolled down his face as he backed up from the game and the crowd. He turned slowly towards Nini and stared into her eyes. Nini stared back, forgetting her conversation with Crow. At least one of her eyes stared back. Her left eye had wandered to the side, as it often did, causing people to double-take and wonder — are you looking at me? If you knew which eye it was, it wasn't a problem. Miguel clearly didn't, and I could see him look back and forth from eye to eye, trying to figure it out.

"Miguel, are you OK?" she asked quietly, so as not to expose him any further to this embarrassing predicament. Without looking back, Meghan squared her legs to the game in a gesture that she had made her decision and was sticking with it.

Miguel let his tear do the talking, then slowly turned and walked out.

Nini stood there for a moment, waiting for someone to do something. When no one did, and everyone just turned back to Meghan and the game, she quietly followed Miguel.

While she was still physically a novice with men, Nini was not a fool to the ways of their minds and manipulations. Aside from our sibling squabbles, she regularly sparred with our emotionally fragile father, who lived down the street in an old redwood carriage barn. He had psychologically knocked Nini many times, mostly for insignificant, childish misdemeanors. A particularly scarring event grew out of a water fight in the front yard. Nini cornered him with the hose and slowly, gleefully marched in, threatening him with jerky spurts. He looked at her round, open face with his dark Mediterranean eyes, pleadingly. A plea for understanding from a child who could not understand his adult fears and pains — for he happened to be suffering in the throes of a decade-long bout of severe paranoia bordering on the schizophrenic — but was all too practiced in forgiving and forgetting them. While he was somehow tangentially aware of his deep fatherly shortcomings, she was still too young and inexperienced to foresee what she would later recognize as the medium of common male communication: his self-worth. But she didn't know this yet.

So she sprayed him. After the soaking, he sprinted into the house and returned with a tomato, which he held in front of her for a moment, letting the suspense build, before he slowly ground it into her 10-year-old face. No explanation necessary. While she hadn't learned to anticipate it, she was quite aware of his see-saw ego by this age, and this scar was only a deeper one among many. She waited until he was done, then slowly walked to the gate and headed for Meghan's house, the seeds dripping from her face proxies for the tears she held back, not willing to let her fragile father see. Not out of pride, but because she didn't want him to feel worse than she imagined he might already feel. She knew his history, that he had been raised in institutions from the age of two. That he had never known his parents, never been shown parental love. She understood his excuse. And she excused him for it.

Nini found Miguel standing in his arena — the old gas station. He was leaning against a wall in the shadows, one leg bent back like a Latin James Dean. He watched her as she looked for him, spotted him, then slowly walked forward, joining him in the shadow, out of view from the arcade and the others. He lowered his head, then tilted his eyes back up to her, trying, with some success, to smolder. She had found what she was looking for.

"He watched me walk up to him from back behind the gas pump. I think he already knew everything that was going to happen. You know in "Star Wars," when they get caught in the tractor beam …?"

Nini and I sat near the potbelly stove in her bus. Our stepfather had brought the little old school bus with him when he had moved in, and parked it in the front yard. He'd spent some time living in it before we met him, so it was well appointed as a bedroom and afforded Nini a bit more privacy than her old room in the house. I had been extremely jealous at first, but had since come to enjoy the flexibility of leaving the house to spend time with Nini in the bus and returning to the house for warmth, food and motherly comfort.

Nini was taking a break from writing a poem in her notebook that she wouldn't let me see. The lights were low, and the door to the little round wood-burner was open. We shared a cigarette, blowing the smoke into the fire. New to smoking, I practiced my inhale.

She relished the telling, already developing her faculty as a storyteller to imply the importance, the real gravity of the "force" that could occur between two people when sexual energy was produced. In this case, a "Star Wars" reference fit the audience perfectly.

"Once you're in it, you can't get out. So you abandon all resistance and give yourself over to absolute pleasure." The *Rocky Horror* reference went over my head. She had just recently seen the movie for the first time, and while she had similarly debriefed me on the sexual happenings in the movie, she had neglected to sing all the lyrics. She instantly realized her mistake and shifted gears, leaving movie references.

"Miguel has animal attraction," she said, taking a long pause to gauge my enthusiasm. After another thought, she quickly scribbled something in the notebook.

"OK," I spat back, a little jealous. While I, too, was in awe of Miguel, and was thrilled with all he had done for the Jammers, I secretly resented that he had so completely taken the spotlight. Nini picked up on this.

"You have it, too." Generous. "But he has experience."

I resisted letting out a fed-up sigh. This would not be the last time Nini would put me in my place for trailing her in belt notches. She continued, happy to have so easily tamped me down while describing her own victory.

"He totally knows what he's doing. All the time. Did you see the tear? The one tear?"

"Yeah. So what happened after you got stuck in his tractor beam?"

"You know when you inhale for the first time …?" she said as she sucked a wisp of smoke up into her nose. "Your first kiss is like inhaling your first drag off a cigarette, except if you didn't have to cough. You get the head rush, but you don't cough. You know?"

I took the cigarette from her hand and took a deep drag, to remind myself. I nodded, satisfied with myself for not coughing.

"But it lasts … the rest of the day."

"You still feel it right now?" I asked, incredulously.

Now she nodded.

"So then what happened?"

She parsed it out, pausing and staring into the dancing flames, as if seeing the past play out in the fire's light.

"He put his tongue in my mouth and kind of licked my tongue and the sides of my cheeks. The insides."

"That's French kissing!" I blurted out, proudly. "Was it gross?"

"No. It felt good. At first I didn't know what he was doing, but then I remembered that that's what 'Frenching' is."

"See …?" As if I were 10 steps ahead of her. "So what did you do?"

"I did it back to him. And he got a boner."

I was shocked. I wasn't quite expecting that.

"Once he realized I would French him back, he got excited," Nini said, seeing my jaw drop. Now she dug in. "He has a big dick."

"Did you touch it?" I asked, wondering how she knew how big a dick had to be to be "big."

"No, but I could feel it pressing against me. He rubbed it up and down on me."

"Through clothes … ?" I asked.

"Yeah …" She trailed off, recalling the moment.

"Then what?"

"He put his arms around me and held me. And we just stood there for a while."

"Was he still rubbing it on you?" I asked, not really wanting to know.

She nodded.

"And then he sang to me. He sang Lionel Richie."

"Are you kidding?" I forced a laugh, trying in vain to ridicule her.

"He sang, 'Hello.' He says it's our song now."

"You hate that song …" I said, leaving the question mark only for myself.

She slowly shook her head.

"Not any more." She was staring into the fire again. I took the last drag from the cigarette and tossed it into the stove. I exhaled softly, so as not to blow the ashes around, and we both watched the butt become engulfed in licking blue-and-red flames.

EVAN.

Nini and I sat huddled together against the back window of the beat-up old Chevy truck. The rusted-out bed was littered with fishing gear that hung down through gaping holes where the sea air had eaten through the steel. Not poles or lures, but nets and rubber buoys. It stank of old fish and cheap beer, which leaked from a dozen or so empty cans as they knocked around like pinballs each time our blitzed driver nearly missed a curve and violently swerved back onto the road.

Nini had just received her driver's permit but could only drive with an adult, and anyway, she didn't have a car, so we still hitchhiked when we needed to get somewhere out of town and our mother couldn't help. We had decided to head south on Hwy 1, along Tomales Bay, past Marshall and its oyster farms to Point Reyes and further into Inverness. Nini was drawn to the people of these little towns and the wooded hills around them, and they were drawn to her. Her slightly pigeon-toed walk and sometimes-wandering eye gave the impression of a girl who could do no harm, at least to others. She was always welcome to crash at somebody's house, always offered a ride to watch the sun go down at Drakes Beach or to watch it come up on Mt. Vision. She was welcome. The same could not be said for me. I was tolerated and generally ignored. But I was 13 and willing to stay to the end of the night, even if I didn't know where I'd be sleeping.

"This guy is drunk off his ass," I shouted over the wind and rattling beer cans. "We should ask him to stop, and get out."

Our driver had nearly missed a hairpin and had careened off the road onto the soft shoulder and was now fishtailing through the dirt, only inches away from an old rusty barbwire fence.

"We're almost there. I don't want to miss everyone and get stuck without a ride to Hearts Desire," Nini yelled back to me as the truck found traction back onto the road.

Another can disappeared through one of the rust holes, then reappeared, bouncing off the road behind us as our driver braked hard into another curve. If Nini was scared, she didn't show it. Instead, she tried in vain to light a cigarette. But her lighter was no match for the wind, and she gave up. I wanted a cigarette, too. I was scared. This guy was wasted. If we flipped, our chances were slim to nil. My fears increased when we lurched into the next corner, and the rear end slipped off the road again. This time the shoulder wasn't so soft. The tire hit a big rock and bounced Nini and me up into the air and nearly out of the truck. I landed on my face and scraped my chin, which started to bleed. I looked up to see if Nini was OK. Her face was frozen in fear. I sat up and banged on the window. The drunk fisherman in the cab didn't respond. Nini turned around and started smacking the window as well.

"We want to get out now! Stop!" she shouted.

"Stop the fucking truck!" I screamed. He didn't turn or respond, but the ride calmed. We hit a straightaway, and he seemed to be placating us. It took us a moment to realize we had arrived in Point Reyes. The fog had rolled in thick, diffusing the storefronts and parked cars we now glided past.

Relieved, Nini took a moment to inspect my bleeding chin.

"It's not that bad," she said. She shrugged and wiped the blood away with my sleeve.

The drunk fisherman swerved into a parking spot in front of the Western bar and stumbled in, forgetting about his passengers still sitting dazed in the bed of his truck. After a moment, Nini lit a cigarette. I put one in my mouth, then leaned in to her. Our cigarettes kissed as hers lent its ember to mine. We sat silently and smoked our cigarettes for a couple of minutes, then I noticed Nini stiffen. She squinted her eyes. At the far end of town, where Main Street abruptly turns to the east and disappears up the hill, a faint hint of orange peeked out through the blanket of fog.

"Bodi," Nini whispered.

"Huh?"

"It's Bodi," she said, louder now, but still somehow to herself.

I looked back down the road and waited as the hint of orange emerged and revealed itself as a 1968 Plymouth Roadrunner. It percolated slowly down the street towards us, its cherry-bomb tailpipe doing its job to alert any passersby of its presence, even as its driver affected an "I-don't-give-a-shit-if-you-know-I'm-here" expression with his arm hanging limply out of the window.

Without taking her eyes off the car, Nini slowly climbed out of the shitty truck, trying not to draw attention to herself. Once on the sidewalk she quickly ducked behind the oversized chrome door mirror and checked her face and hair. It was a mess. The wind had driven her shoulder-length blonde mane into a spun-out, lopsided rat's nest.

I grabbed my skateboard and jumped out of the truck as the Roadrunner pulled into the gravel parking lot across from the bar. The engine came to life and very delicately approached a burnout, but spun the tires only once, displacing just a handful of gravel which spattered against the brick wall of the abandoned building opposite the Western. Then the ignition was killed and the car came to a heaving stop.

Nini emerged from behind the mirror, her blonde hair deftly tamed with a rubber band into a messy — but attractive — pony tail. She walked across the street and leaned into the passenger-side window of the car. I followed a few feet back but didn't dare lean into the window.

Bodi sat behind the wheel, staring straight ahead, his right hand hanging over the steering wheel. He was a round-faced kid, 17 or 18, with black hair worn short on top and longer and very shaggy in back. Not exactly a mullet, more of a grown-out Keith Richards look, but almost a mullet. I guess he was handsome, because everybody said he was "fine," but I didn't really get it. He was quiet and seemed to question his own coolness even as he exuded it. When he smiled, he did so with only one half of his mouth, as if he had had a stroke. The one undeniably cool thing about him was his nick name. Bodi. I don't know how he got it, and I don't know why it was cool. It just was. Everyone knew his name was Rod, and people called him that, but when you wanted to feel good about yourself, or you wanted to impress someone with how cool you were, you called him Bodi. And it worked. Somehow even I felt cooler when I said "Bodi." And not just cooler, but good; it made me feel good. And Bodi knew it. Perhaps that's why he didn't seem to quite believe how cool he was, for while he knew his nickname inspired such feelings, he didn't know why either.

Troy sat shotgun. He was a tall lanky guy with long brown hair and a perpetually stoned smile. His faded and torn Judas Priest '83 tour jersey told the world he was a lifer, a committed hesher, no poser with a store-bought Van Halen shirt and acid-washed jeans.

"You guys going to Hearts Desire?" Nini asked enthusiastically.

Bodi nodded. Troy smiled a toothy grin.

"Who's that little dude with the skate?" Troy motioned to me and the skateboard tucked under my arm.

"My little brother," Nini replied without taking her eyes off of Bodi. She waited for his response, knowing that this was the moment when it would be revealed if my coming would blow her whole plan. Bodi took his time and mulled it over, but before he could respond, Troy jumped out of the car and bounded over to me.

"Hey dude, can I check your skate?"

I handed it to him. He flung it on the ground and pulled a couple of sketchy 360s.

"Your trucks are tight!" he said, gleefully. "Can you Ollie?" He tried a couple, failing, then kicked the board over to me. I snapped an easy Ollie, then popped the board up into my hand. I raised my eyes slowly, knowing the verdict was coming.

"Rad!" Troy yelled. "Are you curling your foot?"

Relieved, I began a quick tutorial for Troy as Nini climbed into the backseat of the car. All was well. We had a ride, and I was not the persona non grata I could have easily been. As Troy practiced his foot curling I watched Nini rest her chin on the back of Bodi's seat as they talked. Bodi smiled and stared out the windshield as Nini studied the side of his face. Finally, Bodi turned to Troy.

"Troy" was all he needed to say. Troy kicked the board to me, then opened the back seat for me to climb in. He jumped in after me and slammed the door as Bodi pulled the car out onto the road.

We headed south out of town, over the old green metal bridge, and hooked a right toward the wooded hills of Inverness. There was a long straightaway ahead of us, and Bodi opened up the Roadrunner. I searched for a seatbelt but found nothing. Nini played it cool and folded her arms over the back seat and rested her chin on them. She smiled at Troy as the speedometer hit 90, then 100. Nini calmly asked Troy to push in the cigarette lighter. I was impressed by her gentle, almost sleepy façade in the face of impending vehicular doom, but I kicked her anyway in a vain hope that she'd ask them to slow down, a request I knew could not come from me.

The lighter popped, and Troy handed it to her. She turned slowly to me and smiled as she lit a cigarette. She studied my face for a moment, and as we looked into each other's eyes I realized that everything — even her little brother — was up for sacrifice this weekend. If it meant impressing Bodi and getting together with him, all was disposable. She would risk everything to give him everything. Nini had come here to lose her virginity, and she was willing to die in a horrible car crash if that's what it took. She made all of this plain to me with a long, undistracted look into my eyes. I took the lighter from her hand and lit my own cigarette. I took a long drag and then looked out the side window at the trees flying past, a forced calm now settling over me. Satisfied, Nini threw her arms back over the seat and once again rested her chin on them.

As Bodi finally let the car idle to a more comfortable 70, I wondered why Nini had brought me. She was clearly on a mission, and while I had been momentarily accepted by the older guys it could have just as easily gone the other way — we both could have been tossed aside because I was a little grommet who would no doubt drink a lot of their beer and probably throw up in the car. She could have easily upped her chances and come alone. Perhaps she was, despite all outward appearances, actually nervous about her quest were it to come to fruition … ? Might I be comfort for her during the possible occasion of a major life milestone? Maybe she thought that even though I was no match physically for Bodi — being much younger and smaller — perhaps I could muster some defense if things were to get out of hand once they got down to business. This seemed unlikely. Why would she be worried about that kind of thing? She was willing to die in a fiery wreck for the chance to be with him. I shrugged it off and looked out the window at the rolling green hills of the far side of the bay, reflected in its still water.

We pulled into the parking lot at Heart's Desire and climbed out.

"Evan's here," Nini said, pointing to a Chevy stepside pickup. We followed Bodi and Troy down the dark, wooded path towards the beach below.

A bonfire was already blazing, and 15 or so townies were drinking beer, smoking and playing the odd guitar. I stayed back to survey the scene as Nini followed the boys over to a blanket near the fire where Kallie, a large punky-looking girl of 16 or so, sat drinking a wine cooler. Kallie and Nini chatted and lit cigarettes. Curiously, Bodi lingered nearby awkwardly glancing towards Nini, who seemed to have forgotten all about him. I waved at a couple of kids I kind of knew, and sat down on some driftwood that was conveniently placed next to someone's unguarded 12-pack.

I slipped my hand into the box but found it was empty. The kids I kind of knew watched and snickered at me.

Fuckers. Blood draining from my embarrassed head, I turned my attention back to Nini and watched as Bodi circled her. She was now comfortably encamped on Kallie's Mexican throw blanket, chatting away about UB40 and completely unaware of Bodi's travails. Ignored, Bodi finally marched off to where Troy and a couple other stoners had started a game of hacky sack, and joined in.

Nini turned her head ever so slightly, and I realized she had been aware of Bodi the entire time. How and when had she become so sophisticated in her approach? Generally, Nini wore life on her sleeve. If she liked you, you knew it. She had come on pretty strong in town and in the car. Now it seemed she was switching gears into hard-to-get… But this was different. She was working on a big project, not just trying to get Evan or Joe Shmo to make out with her in the back of their car. This was her virginity. She had chosen her man, and now she was working to achieve her goal. And so far I thought she was doing a pretty good job.

She shared a bit more smalltalk with Kallie, then got up and walked over to where Evan was standing, bare feet in water, smoking a joint and staring out over the darkening bay.

She glanced over at Bodi, who quickly glanced back, then she took her shoes off, rolled up her jeans and stepped into the water next to Evan. Evan's long blond hair briefly blew back in the wind comically, so as to appear to be horizontal. He held it down with one hand and as the water lapped over her feet, Nini fell in next to him and they shared a laugh and his joint. Nini and Evan had "gotten together" many times, and she liked him, but she complained that he liked her too much, a notion I was not sure I fully understood.

After a minute or two they were joined by Bodi. Nini passed Bodi the joint. I was impressed that Evan didn't seem to mind. These were cool people, generally, and Nini knew they were. And they knew she was. Whatever happened, passing a joint around wasn't going to spark jealousy or greed. Weed was shared, period.

Mona sat down beside me on the log, dropping a six-pack into the sand between her legs. My heart rate went through the roof. At 14, Mona was the only girl in this crowd who was remotely in my strata of possibilities, though she had never presented as such before. Many parties just like this one had passed in which Mona had not even noticed that I was there. She didn't come off as a kid. She was young, but while I was a grommet, a little punk, she was one of them. No one differentiated between her and the rest of the pack. I was not so fortunate. But here she was, sitting next to me. I turned to her, panicking. She smiled with her full, red lips. It was a kind smile, which surprised me, because while I longed for even a glance from her, I had always imagined that a close encounter with her would reveal her to be a horrible bitch. I was wrong. Kind of.

"You're Nini's brother, right?" she purred. Her voice was low and soft, and she had a calculated — perhaps manufactured — way of moving her mouth, which of course drew my eyes to it, which perhaps was the point. Not that I cared. She was like a warm blanket swirling around me.

"Yeah. What's your name?" I asked, knowing full well what her name was. She smiled. She knew I knew. She didn't answer, just looked away towards the gently lapping waves. I looked over her short black dress, her tan legs. Her shoulder-length black hair curled up just at the end, vaguely suggesting a '60s flip. She turned back to me and perhaps caught me studying her knees.

"You want a beer?" She didn't wait for me to answer, placing a cold can of Miller in my lap. Damn. Is this really happening? I asked myself.

"Thanks." I opened the beer and we sat for a moment, sipping.

"Your chin is bleeding."

I mopped it with my sleeve.

We both watched as Nini swayed between Evan and Bodi. I could see from her body language that she had changed her approach. She was no longer using Evan to lure Bodi, she was choosing between the two. And it looked like the choice was hers to make.

"Which one do you think she likes more?" Mona pondered aloud. She was sharp, this 14-year-old. Sharp enough to know she was a full year older than me? I couldn't tell. She was sitting with me, talking to me, but she hadn't answered when I asked her name. Maybe she just didn't play games? She had just tossed a beer in my lap. She was pretty straightforward. How would she respond to me putting my hand on her leg? Or grazing her finger with mine? Or smiling at her? I looked over at the kids I was glad I didn't know better just long enough to let them know I knew they knew I was sitting with this girl, the only girl. Once I was sure they knew, I turned back to Mona. She was watching Nini so I joined her. To my surprise Nini and Evan turned and left Bodi standing in the water, tiny waves biting at his ankles. They picked up their shoes and walked over to us.

"Evan's got the new Elvis Costello tape in his car, we're going to listen to it," Nini said, giving me just enough of a look to let me know there was no need to follow.

"Bodi hates Elvis Costello," she said, letting me know Bodi wouldn't be following, either.

"Cool," I responded, then looked back at her just long enough to let her know I was freaking out about Mona. Nini turned to Mona as Evan and I shared a congenial nod.

"Hey, Mona. Take care of my little brother for a bit?"

Mona smiled and nodded. I looked down and tried not to shake my head as a wave of embarrassment washed over my face.

"Already on it, Nini," Mona said, letting her voice pitch higher in a slightly jokey way.

"Spare a beer?" Evan asked Mona. She tossed him one as if she'd tossed a hundred beers to 17-year-olds at beach parties. Evan and Nini headed up the now very-dark path through the trees to the parking lot. I turned back to Mona. She looked into my eyes.

"I'm cold," she said as she squinted her eyes and melted my brain. How to respond to this? Give her my jacket? Put my arm around her? She was in a short sleeveless dress. The wind had come up again and it was getting cold, but any offering that could be misconstrued might tank any chances I had … . I looked down and thought. I could feel her waiting.

"Want to go stand by the fire?" she asked as she stood up. Damn. I had taken too long to respond.

"Yeah," I blurted out as I followed her over to the fire where she sat down next to Bodi, who was warming his wet feet.

"What's up Bodi?" She sounded cool indeed …

I awkwardly sat down next to her, kicking some sand onto her dress. She brushed the sand away, but she might as well have been brushing me away. I could feel my chances slip away as she and Bodi exchanged some small talk that reeked of foreshadowing.

"Would you grab me the last beer? I left it over by the log we were sitting on." The purr was gone, replaced by a strident, pitying coldness. In one brief moment, I had lost.

"Sure." I quickly ran for the beer, knocking more sand onto her dress and revealing myself through my eagerness as the child I still was. By the time I got to the beer and turned back, Bodi had made his move, putting his arm around Mona's bare shoulder. Her head fell onto him and crushed my soul. I watched with utter devastation as the curled tips of her shiny black hair fell down his back. I walked back over and dropped the beer next to her. She smiled up from Bodi's shoulder, the reflection of the bonfire burning in her eyes. He looked up, too, smiling with half his mouth. Their kindness made my stomach turn.

"Thanks …" she purred again, but now the purr was for Bodi. I looked at her one last time, then wandered away from the fire toward the dark path that led up to the parking lot.

"Don't wander too far off," she said with a motherly tone that twisted the dagger-like words into my guts. Take care of me, indeed.

I pretended not to hear and continued up the path into the canopy. It was night now, and the sounds of the forest grew loud as I left the others behind and was swallowed by the darkness.

"You are such a retard," Nini jabbed. "She was totally into you."

"All I did was take like two seconds too long to answer her," I replied defiantly.

"You gotta know when to hold 'em, know when to fold 'em."

"I hate Kenny Rogers," I lamented.

"Me too, but he's right." She turned and looked out the side window at the bay. We were in the back seat of a 1970s Cadillac DeVille, driven by a middle-aged man with a huge potbelly, on top of which he rested a can of Coors and a cigarette in the same hand. He had picked us up about a half-mile north of Point Reyes, which is as far as we had walked that morning, after starting at Evan's house at around 6:30, before his parents awoke. The wet eucalyptus that lined the road had dropped fresh-smelling dew on us as we walked, and we were feeling fairly refreshed after what had turned out to be a pretty serious night of drinking, smoking, and in Nini's case, screwing.

We were on the other side of the bay now from Hearts Desire, and Nini was looking across, perhaps hoping to somehow summon herself of the night before, the ghost of the Virgin Nini, during her conquest and ultimate transformation. Was it a transformation? Could sex change someone that drastically as to make them a new person? Was that girl she searched for in the distance a different girl perhaps than the one that sat next to me now?

"So?" I demanded. She smiled.

"It didn't hurt as much as Meghan said it would."

"Did you like it?" I asked, knowing the flood was coming.

Our driver checked us in the rearview mirror. Nini leaned in closer and lowered her voice.

"Not really … the first time." Her eyes smiled. "He had to push his dick really hard to get in and I just had to kind of sit there and wait, but then I helped with my hand. I just spread my lips out. But I only had to do that once. After that I guess I loosened up because he got it in pretty easily."

"What? How many times did you do it?" I asked incredulously.

"Three times. Once in the truck, when you were yelling for me."

"I knew you heard me!"

"He was totally fucking me, you think I was going to be like, I'm over here, getting fucked?"

"I don't know," I shrugged.

"That's because you're a virgin."

I looked at her and cocked my head. She laughed.

"Well you are. And I'm not. That's the difference between us now."

"Not for long."

"You could have lost it last night with Mona if you weren't such a retard."

"Fuck you. So you did it in the truck, pretending not to hear me, then what?" I asked, intent on getting the story.

"Then after we got to Evan's, and you fell asleep, we did it in the closet in his room. Standing up."

"How does that even work?" I honestly could not imagine.

"And then this morning we did it in bed, before you woke up. That's when I finally liked it. Way better in a bed," she bragged.

"So how come you picked Evan, not Bodi? I totally thought you were going to get together with Bodi."

Nini thought for a moment. "I wanted to feel safe. When I was standing in the water, next to Evan, I felt safe. I knew I could trust him." She looked out the window. I pondered this, coming to the conclusion that this was an excellent — though surprising — reason. She had seemed completely worry-free going 100 miles per hour in Bodi's car.

"Bodi is … he's kind of dangerous, I think," she said, as her lip curled into just the slightest smile.

The driver turned back and looked Nini over. We both sat quietly for the next few minutes, hoping things were not going to get weird. The driver was silent for a time, too, until finally he coughed out, "How old are you two, anyway?" Nini and I looked at each other, acknowledging that it had just gotten weird.

"We're underage." I said, raising my voice so it could not be mistaken. He flicked his cigarette out the window and turned back to us again, looking us over. A curve loomed ahead. We both waited for him to turn back, but he was really looking Nini over now, whetting his lips.

"Dude, watch the road!" I shouted. He turned back to

the road and slid the car into the curve, crossing the yellow line. We hit some gravel and the back end cut loose. The old perv knew how to drive. He spun the wheel into the curve and drifted the car back into control. As we rounded the corner we could see the little houses of Tomales ahead, few as they were, and knew we were nearly home.

BODI.

I could see the Roadrunner sitting downtown from the back porch of our house, even though it was still a good half-mile away. Nini sat next to me on the swinging bench, and I could feel her begin to vibrate in her seat as the Plymouth's headlights turned on, glowing ominously in the thin fog. We could see the cloud of smoke from the spinning tires before we could hear the squeal, and soon the car was racing up the hill toward us.

Nini had cut her hair to a more modern shoulder-length soon after losing her virginity, in an effort — I suppose — to physically manifest the change she felt so strongly inside, and she was now checking her hair in the reflection of the window beside us, sweeping it to one side with her hand.

"Do I look cool?" she asked, expecting an affirmation.

"Yeah," I replied, honestly. I thought she did. I thought she was the coolest chick I knew, and I didn't mind her knowing it. She had cut it shorter in the front, too, and the last vestiges of the country-girl look she had long maintained were gone. She looked like she was from "town."

I walked her to the heavy front gate and held it open for her. Our younger sister emerged at the front door and watched with a toothy grin through the panes. Even she knew what was afoot. Nini stepped onto the thin strip of gravel that separated our hedge from Hwy 1. I heard the rumbling of the big block V8 approaching and stepped out beside her.

Bodi pulled the big car over to our side of the road and put it in park. That he was sitting on the opposite side of the road on a blind hill at dusk didn't seem to bother him, but Nini and I both felt the urgency of possible calamity should a speeding car, or worse yet, a semi-truck, come barreling over the hill.

"What's up, Nini?" Bodi slurred from the car, his half-smile partially obscuring his somewhat pointy teeth.

"Hey, Bodi," she replied, as she fiddled with her hair. "What's up?"

"You told me you wanted to go for a drive …"

"Yeah …" Nini said, as she looked toward the blind hill. It made her anxious, but she didn't want to blow it by rushing things. She wanted to go for a drive.

"Where?" Bodi asked, which seemed a silly question to me — after all, wasn't it obvious this was more about parking than it was driving? Even our younger sister knew this was about "getting together." Maybe he was playing it cool.

"I don't care."

Bodi shrugged, then looked at me.

"You comin'?" he asked me. A question I thought not necessary. He's not playing it cool at all, I thought to myself. He has no idea what he's got coming.

"He can't," Nini answered, as she pushed me out of the way and made her way around the car. Bodi reached over and unlocked the door, and she climbed in. She waved as Bodi half-smiled at me.

"Later." He dropped the car into drive and stepped on

it, spitting gravel across the road and into the back of my head as I dove for cover. I turned back just in time to see him cross the road as a Winnebago came up over the hill, missing the Roadrunner by a hair.

"Bodi likes head," Nini said as she brushed her teeth. I had already brushed and was standing in the doorway of the bathroom, leaning against the jam. It was late for a school night, maybe 10 o'clock. I had heard the rumble of Bodi's Plymouth around 9:30 and waited for 20 minutes for Nini to come in, the car loudly idling the whole time.

"Head?" I asked.

"Blowjob," she said, spitting out the toothpaste.

I didn't respond. I only vaguely knew what a blowjob was and had often wondered how and when "blowing" was involved. It just didn't make sense.

"That's all he wanted," Nini finally said as she wiped her mouth.

"And you did it?"

"Outside, right before I came in," she said and walked out of the bathroom. I followed her out to the bus. She flicked on the light, illuminating the David Bowie "Let's Dance" poster she had recently acquired on a trip to the Santa Rosa mall with Franny, a girl from school who she'd lately become friendly with, presumably because she wasn't a virgin anymore, and neither was Franny. But I wasn't sure.

"Where'd you guys go?" I asked, as I sat down on her bed and began to crumple up some old newspaper to use for fire starter in the potbelly stove.

"We drove up to Elephant Rock. Bodi almost fell off the rock 'cause it was so slippery from the fog. We went in the little cave and were making out when these hicks showed up and started shooting bottles with a .22."

I was impressed she knew the caliber of the gun.

"Bodi got scared and we hid in the cave for like an hour,

waiting for them to leave. I tried to get him to fuck me in the cave, but he couldn't get it up. I guess he was too scared. But then it turned out he only wanted a blowjob, so maybe that was why."

I pondered this surprising take on Bodi. He was one of the coolest guys we knew. He couldn't get it up except for a blowjob? What did this mean? Did it make him less cool? What about Mona? Had she given him a blowjob? And what of it?

"Is it fun?" I asked, earnestly.

"What?"

"Giving a blowjob."

"Why, you want to give it a try?" she asked. She giggled.

"No," I replied, trying to mask my embarrassment. "I'm just curious."

"My jaw got kind of tired. You have to keep your mouth open without using your teeth. I used my teeth at first and he got pissed. But then I figured it out I guess, 'cause I made him cum."

I grimaced.

"In your mouth?"

She laughed and nodded. "But I spit it out. He told me next time I should swallow. It feels better for the guy."

I just stood there and watched as Nini prepared for bed, obviously pleased with herself. She was having a breakout so she rubbed her face vigorously with some kind of medicated pad.

"Is it fun, though? As fun as sex?" I wondered aloud.

"It is sex … . It's not as fun as … regular sex …" She thought for a moment. "But I guess it's fun. Probably gets more fun the more you do it …"

And I guess it was, because Nini gave Bodi head a lot. So much that he began to call her the "Head Master," a term that, while she kept it a secret from all but me, she was very proud of. Evidently it was something she did very well, and Bodi would drive up the bay road at least once a week for the next year or so to get it. She would often recount the details to me, but I grew tired of the stories, as they began to sound the same. Bodi would pick her up, they'd drive somewhere, and she'd give him a blowjob. Not terribly interesting after the 10th or 11th time, even for a horny 13-year-old eager for any scrap of sexual knowledge.

And then he stopped coming. Nini couldn't understand what had happened. She had invested so much in pleasing him, giving him everything he wanted. Now she waited in vain for him to shine on her again, but he didn't. He just stopped coming. She would call, and write him letters. She wrote him poems. She would beg the stars for his attention, but he had moved on.

We saw him at a party, on Mt. Vision, that Franny had brought us to. At first all was cool. Nini and Franny were quite a pair — two short blondes looking for action. Then Bodi showed up. Nini shotgunned a beer and mustered enough courage to confront him. But he ignored her. She shotgunned another and began to beg for an answer why. Why had he stopped coming to see her? Why wouldn't he talk to her? He just smiled with his half-smile and said, "Get over it." Nini responded by getting very drunk.

"Was I an idiot last night?" Nini asked, her head in her hands.

"You don't remember?"

She looked up at me. "What did I do?"

"You don't remember anything?"

"I remember giving someone a blowjob. I think it was Bodi. And I remember throwing up."

"It wasn't Bodi."

She waited for more, pain in her face.

"You begged Bodi to let you suck his dick."

"Oh my God. How do you know? I did it in front of you?"

"You were following him around, begging him. In front of everyone."

He had laughed at her, in her face. I left that out.

"I was begging him to let me suck his dick … ? In front of everyone?" She could barely say the words.

I nodded. "I tried to stop you."

"I think I'm going to puke."

I sat silently as she put her head in her hands again, trying to get her bearings.

"So what happened?" she asked without looking up.

"Well … after you stopped begging Bodi …"

"So he just said 'no'? To me begging?"

"Pretty much." I left out the laughing again.

"Then what happened?"

"It gets worse."

"Fuck … . Tell me."

"You were … pretty much … offering to suck anyone's dick …" I said, as I thought back to the night before. Nini had finally gotten angry with Bodi and had shouted at him. She had called him a scumbag and chastised him for not being able to fuck, just get his dick sucked. This had wiped the smile off his face and got him to stop laughing, at least. After that Nini had basically made it clear she'd suck anyone's dick just to show Bodi up. A guy named Rich who I didn't really know had taken her up on it, and they'd gotten into his Camaro for 15 or 20 minutes. I sat nearby and kept an eye on the car. When she got out, she threw up on the hood of the car, then climbed into the back of Franny's truck where she'd stayed until Franny dropped us off at home early the next morning.

I summed it up for Nini. "… and you ended up giving some guy named Rich a blowjob in his car, then you puked, then you passed out in Franny's truck."

Nini got up and went to her bus. I didn't see her for the rest of the day. Later that evening, when I poked my head into the bus, she was asleep in bed. The next morning I checked again. She was still asleep. And the same that afternoon. Finally, I gently shook her. She opened her eyes, but they were dark, vacant.

"Hey … you OK?"

"No."

"You should get up."

"No."

She shut her eyes again.

The next morning I went out to the bus again. She was up. She sat next to the little potbelly stove, with an electric hair trimmer in her hands. Piles of hair surrounded her on the floor.

"What are you doing?" I asked in horror.

She looked up.

"Changing. Changing into something Bodi would never want." She dropped her head again and continued shaving.

"Want some help?"

She looked up at me.

"Can you do the back? I can't see."

I got down on the floor and took the buzzer. She put her head down, and I began to clean up the mess that was the back of her head.

"Thanks."

"No problem."

MARCUS.

You're still a virgin," Nini whispered in my ear, her overly hair-sprayed New Wave hairdo bumping me in the head.

"She gave me a blowjob," I spat back, defensively.

"Blowjobs don't count." She smiled and looked out the window at the passing fields of green grass and cows. Our mother sang a quiet song to our younger sister from the driver's seat, unconcerned by our preoccupation with sex.

"They always did for you," I whined.

"If you get a blowjob because you're scared to have real sex, then you're still a virgin," Nini explained. She was right. At Nini's request we had recently stopped going to school in Tomales and started attending a hippie school in a log cabin situated down a long dirt road near Sebastopol. Nini had demanded it, explaining that she refused to go to school with anyone who knew Bodi or had been at the party where she had begged him.

Changing schools had dramatically expanded the pool of potential sexual partners for both Nini and me. Making out had become so routine and easy to come by for me that I had begun, at Nini's behest, to get to second and third bases, and in one case, had wound up on the school roof with a ninth-grader named Sasha who was more than willing to "take" my virginity. As we fumbled with removing our jeans, I fearfully explained to her that the roof was made of a rough material and I worried that she may get a rash on her ass from it, so I demurred and suggested she give me a blowjob instead.

"You have to put your penis in her vagina, and come. Everyone knows that," Nini said, smirking. Holding this inequity over my head had become a favorite pastime for her on the daily ride to school.

"Well, Sasha gives good head," I said, trying to avoid eye contact.

"How would you know?"

"Because my sister is the 'Head Master.' I've heard all about what makes good head," I whispered in her face, for effect.

She paused. She had been proud of this moniker, but after the Mt. Vision debacle it had begun to sting. She had recently questioned the whole notion of giving blowjobs when one of the hippie girls at school had revealed that they considered giving head anti-feminist. When I insisted that the girl only said it because she was ugly, Nini had slugged me in the arm.

"Well, you're still a virgin," she said as we pulled onto the dirt road that led to the tiny school.

More so than she knew, for while technically Sasha *had* put my dick in her mouth, she had only done it for a brief moment before deciding she didn't want to give me a blowjob and climbing down off the roof. I knew I had blown it. Sasha was totally willing. She had slept with at least two of my friends and had done so with no strings attached, just for fun. I had developed a paralyzing fear of not being able to pull off real sex and so had invented the rough-roof defense. Idiot.

"What's up, dude?" Marcus asked from the front step. He was dressed in all black, with a skateboard under his arm and eyeliner under his eyes. He didn't really skate, but liked the skater crowd so carried one most days. At 16, he was a couple of years older than me, but we had bonded over skating, and I considered him my first — and so far only — true friend at the school.

"Went to a party in Petaluma over the weekend. Dale Dork was there," I bragged. But Marcus had already lost interest. His eyes were on Nini now, or on her hair. It was something of a mohawk, shaved on the sides and back, with the entirety of hair from the top of her head standing straight up and cascading forward. Not terribly dissimilar to the bride of Frankenstein's 'do, but in reverse. She wore an old surplus army jacket, jeans and China flats — thin, black canvas shoes with plastic soles you could pick up in Chinatown for a couple of bucks.

Nini stepped up next to Marcus, and he put his arm around her; a move that surprised me, as Nini generally told me everything, and this was a clear sign things had developed without my knowledge. She had not mentioned even kissing him, let alone "going out." I followed them into the school.

At the morning meeting, while the entire faculty and student body, totaling maybe 50, sat around the deck of the cabin, Nini and Marcus sat to the side, making out and sharing a cigarette. I didn't begrudge Marcus for throwing me over for Nini, but I couldn't understand how this had gotten so serious without my knowledge. I felt a slight sense of betrayal and couldn't wait until I could get Nini alone and grill her about it.

At lunch I sat waiting on the steps, but she didn't show up. Every day since our arrival at the school we had dined together on the steps, a solid bloc of newcomer attitude. But today I was alone. As the tie-dye teacher called out that lunch was over, I saw Nini and Marcus emerge from the trees below the school, along with a couple of other kids.

When school let out I waited by the steps again and this time Nini did show up as usual, but she was again with Marcus.

"Marcus is coming over. So is Amenita," Nini said loudly as she walked by, hand-in-hand with Marcus, Amenita trailing behind them.

We all piled into Marcus' Peugeot wagon — Marcus driving, of course, with Nini beside him riding shotgun, and me in the back seat beside Amenita.

Amenita was a short, round Jewish girl with a big nose and big boobs. She was squarely in my age bracket, and I couldn't help but wonder if Nini had arranged for her to come on my behalf. While Nini loved to rib me about my lack of sexual experience, she was squarely in my corner and did what she could to facilitate anyway she could. I had hardly spoken to Amenita, but we did share a math class so I felt enabled.

"Do you like math?" I asked feebly, then noticed Nini's hand resting on Marcus' leg.

"I guess so," Amenita replied. "Do you like math?" she continued, sarcastically.

"I guess so," I replied, feeling doomed. Looking for a deflection, I leaned forward.

"Can I have a smoke?" I asked Nini. She pulled the pack from her pocket and lit one for me, took a drag, then passed it back. I leaned back with the cigarette and stared forward, taking small drags and trying not to touch Amenita's bare legs, which were splayed about haphazardly.

Amenita gently laid her hand on mine, fingered my smoke and slid it out of my hand. Reeling from the electricity of the still-uncommon female touch, I watched as she brought it up to her mouth and took a long drag. Our eyes met and she French-inhaled, then blew a smoke ring in my face. She handed the cigarette back to me and busted up laughing. Nini looked back at me, and we shared a quizzical look.

In Nini's bus that night we all sat around the little potbelly stove and shared a 40-ounce bottle of malt liquor. Our mother had taken our little sister with her to her Sufi meeting, so we were unattended. Not that it mattered, as the old hippie bus had afforded her, and me when allowed, almost total autonomy.

"I think I'm drunk," Amenita sputtered. I looked at her incredulously. We were all sharing one bottle. I looked at Nini, and my suspicions were corroborated. She motioned outside, but I couldn't figure out what she meant.

"You should get some fresh air, Amenita. Maybe some water," Nini said, looking at me the whole time. Now I got it.

"I can show you where …" I blurted out.

"OK," Amenita quickly replied.

We stepped out into the cool, foggy air. It was dark so she put her hand in my back pocket and followed me to the house. Inside, I got her a glass of water. She drank it down, keeping her eyes fixed on mine.

"Are you a virgin?" she asked as she wiped some water off her chin. I froze. After a moment of mental math, I shook my head. I realized that Nini had probably told her I was, when she convinced her to come home with us. But I just couldn't bring myself to admit it.

"No." I looked away, unable to lie directly into her eyes.

"That's too bad," she replied, after a moment of consideration. "Because I really want to have sex with a virgin … or something weird."

I squirmed, knowing now how bad I'd blown it by lying. I strained to think of something to say, some comeback, something weird to offer. A blowjob? Not weird. Anal? Definitely not. Just make out? Kid stuff.

She stood there waiting for a reply, drinking her water. I said nothing. Finally, she put the glass down and went to the door.

"I'm gonna see what your sister and Marcus are doing," she said, then turned and walked out.

"You dumbfuck!" Nini shouted at me over breakfast the next morning.

"Mom!" Our little sister complained to our mother.

"Nini, don't speak like that at the table."

"Idiot." She leaned into me. "I handed her to you on a silver platter."

"I know. I just …"

"The whole reason she came over was because I told her you were a virgin. She totally wanted to deflower you."

"Where did she go?" Little sister asked.

"She left with Marcus. If she fucks Marcus again, I'm gonna kill you," she said, pointing at me.

"Again?" I wondered aloud.

"When she came back to the bus, Marcus and I were in bed; she just climbed right in."

I sat there, aghast. This had never occurred to me. "You mean … ?"

"Ménage à trois," Nini said, putting just a hint of French accent on it for effect. "Marcus has a huge dick."

"What does that have to do with it?" I asked.

"There was plenty to go around." She smiled to herself, then got up and walked to the fridge, bow-legged and limping for effect.

"Give me a break," I said as she grabbed the milk and walked back, sans limp.

My mother had left the room, so Nini leaned in with the details as she sat back down.

"Amenita has no gag reflex. She deep-throated him. His dick is like this." She held her hands nearly a foot apart. "I had to use lube just to get it in."

I tried not to show the absurd amount of jealousy I felt.

"So you let her give him a blowjob while you were getting together with him?"

"Yep. We did a little kissing show for him, to get him super hard …"

"OK, stop!" I shouted. "I don't want to hear it."

"You blew it so bad. You shouldn't have lied. She would have put your whole dick in her mouth. She would have fucked you all night."

I dropped my head and stared at my cereal.

"You guys are so gross," said our little sister.

"I'm not. I didn't do anything," I said, still looking down into the bowl.

JERRY.

A sly grin spread across his face as he watched Nini and Meghan smoking cigarettes by the post office. No longer pursuing a punk look, Nini had grown her hair back out to shoulder length, while Meghan had cut hers into a short pixie cut. They both wore Birkenstocks. Jerry leaned easily against his truck — a mid-'70s Ford that was battered but sturdy, his right leg bent back and resting on its bumper. He wore a puffer vest over a t-shirt, Levi's and brown work boots. His longish brown hair curled up at his collar and swept back over his ears. His flat, wide-open face grinned easily, always with a fox's studiousness. He was quiet, only spoke when it seemed important enough to do so and laughed easily. While everyone knew Jerry, or at least knew his name, no one was quite sure who he really was, who his parents were or where he came from. He had kind of seeped into our world. At 21 he was among the oldest of us kids and was the only among us to have his own place — a small cottage on Tomales Bay, in the tiny townlet of Marshall. He was not a fisherman, though he lived among the small throng of men who still fished the bay and beyond, and they seemed to consider him one of their own.

Nini didn't notice him at first, I don't think. Perhaps, given the five-year gap between them, he seemed too old or too calm. She was occasionally servicing Bodi again, something we did not speak about. He would pick her up and she would return, just like before, but now there were no details. She was also maintaining a friendship with Marcus that included occasional hookups.

Jerry noticed her, and I noticed him noticing her. He seemed to be a man among children. I watched as he would pull into town, survey the scene of a few teenagers hanging around in front of the store after school. He would watch from his truck for a while, casually chatting with someone through the window. Then he would open the door, swing a leg out. Rest there for a while, always watching, grinning and nodding, listening … taking it in. Then he might slowly walk into the store and buy a coke, leaving his truck door open. Often he would return to find a kid sitting in the truck, messing with the radio. Jerry liked hippie music — the Grateful Dead, Bob Dylan. He'd come back to find some kid had changed the station to Top 40. But he didn't mind. He'd take it as a cue to walk around to the back of the truck, lean against the tailgate, put a leg up and watch.

Nini did finally notice him. On a particularly slow day after school he had shown up with a dressed deer, freshly killed, in the back of his truck. He could only stop for a few minutes, as he wanted to get the deer hung as soon as possible, and so bought a bottle of soda and quickly drank it while the rest of us ogled his kill. Nini was shocked by the bloody carcass lying there in the truck, its eye staring its death stare in an awkward direction. She self-consciously checked the mirror to see if her eye, too, was drifting. It wasn't. She was by now a self-avowed vegetarian. Not an animal-lover per-se, but she was empathetic to anything that breathed and could no longer stomach meat.

"Are you going to eat it?" Nini asked Jerry, doing her best to avoid sounding accusatory.

"Some of it," he said, his dry, reedy voice pinching in anticipation of the kids growing disgusted with him for "murdering" the poor deer or something. But this did not come about.

"That's good," said Nini. They shared the briefest of looks between them, but it was on. "At least it didn't die for nothing."

Jerry silently nodded as Nini looked him over, gauging his reaction, his empathy.

"Did you know Jerry has his own house?" Nini asked as we walked up the hill to our house from downtown.

"Everybody knows that," I responded, happy to know something she didn't, or had just learned, anyway.

"How old is he?" she asked.

"Twenty one."

"How do you know?"

"I've seen him buy beer," I replied.

She nodded, and we continued on, silently. I knew where she was going with this, and she knew I knew, so there was no need to discuss it any further.

The next day, after school, Nini didn't smoke with Meghan. She stood around, idly looking at her reflection in the large plate-glass windows of the general store. This was somewhat out of character for her. She was no narcissist. She was insecure about her looks and her body, often grabbing handfuls of flesh from her waist and pretending to cut them off with scissors. Her skin was also a constant source of self-loathing. But while I knew firsthand that these shortcomings caused her great pain, they never got in the way of romance. They were a personal battle she fought at home, not in public. So it was strange to now watch her looking in the glass, judging herself.

Of course she had already made an impression on Jerry, a big one. I had been watching him watch her for weeks. I was surprised it had taken her this long to notice him, but he was really too old for her. Too old to be hanging out with us at all.

When Jerry finally pulled up, Nini played it very cool. She had positioned herself on the high curb near where he usually parked so that as he pulled in he had to acknowledge her by slowing down and not pulling completely in, peering over the hood at her as he slowed to a stop a couple feet away. She watched him calmly as he did so, defiant of the danger his truck imposed on her.

As he sat in the cab, chatting with Crow about something or other, he and Nini exchanged glances. When he got out and went into the store, Nini stayed put, pretending to ignore his absence. She chatted with Grace, another local girl with dazzling blue eyes that always seemed on the verge of tears. When Jerry returned, he brought two RC colas. He sat down next to Nini and offered her one. Grace took the cue and wandered off into the post office where Crow and Meghan's older sister, Abby, were studying the FBI's most-wanted posters. Nini accepted the bottle and they both checked under their caps for a winning code for a game RC was then running. Neither having won, Jerry flicked his cap across the street. Nini smiled and handed him hers, and he flicked it as well. I watched them from up the curb a bit, where I sat on my skateboard shooting the shit with Celia, a tomboy who was completely — at least to my knowledge — oblivious to things romantic.

When Nini got in Jerry's truck, she looked back at me, letting me know she'd be home late. I waved, acknowledging the communiqué, then stood up to go.

"What's that all about?" Celia asked me as the others

filed out of the post office. I shrugged and walked up the hill alone.

"We laid on a white sheepskin rug in front of the fire. His house is right on the water, on stilts, so you can hear the tiny waves of the bay lapping underneath. It's so romantic," Nini recalled as she flossed her teeth — something she had recently started to do after a particularly bad dentist's visit. She spoke haltingly, between teeth.

"Romantic?" I asked incredulously from the edge of the toilet where I sat, conspicuously not flossing my teeth. Nini was not one to wax poetic about "romance." She was a brass-tacks, teenage sex queen. The word "romantic" sounded totally out of place coming out of her mouth.

She stopped flossing and looked at me.

"He didn't even try to fuck me. We drank wine and made tiny paper airplanes and flew them into the fire and watched them burn," she said, then started flossing again. "He plays bass."

"Seems like a bass player, actually," I said, meaning it. I pictured him turkey-necking on stage to "Sugar Magnolia."

"Did you even kiss?"

She shook her head "no."

"Tomorrow we're going to the movies in town."

"Can I come?" I asked, fully expecting "no" to be the answer.

"Yeah, he actually invited you, too. He said, 'Bring your brother if you want.'"

"Are you serious?" I expected her to bust up laughing. But she just nodded.

"Unh-huh," she murmured through the floss.

I smiled. "Thanks."

She smiled back as she unwound the floss from her fingers and tossed it in the trash.

I sat in the back of the truck on the way to Petaluma.

Nini sat in the cab with Jerry, of course. Close, but not touching. I watched through the back window as they chatted, smiling and occasionally laughing. Jerry didn't smoke, but he let her smoke in his truck, and she did. I tried to light a smoke myself but couldn't get my lighter to light in the wind, so I gave up.

We sat in a row in the movie theater, Nini in the middle. It was strange, grownup. Jerry bought us both popcorn and drinks. He acted more like a dad than a boyfriend. And Nini acted grownup, too. As if taking a cue from Jerry, she held herself more like an adult. She spoke less, and when she did speak it was measured, thoughtful. I felt like a little kid. But I was happy for her. She really liked Jerry, I could tell, even though it was early in their relationship.

As the theater darkened, she put her hand on Jerry's leg. I watched out of the corner of my eye as he did nothing. She looked at him, waiting for a response. Finally, he turned to her and grinned, just a hint of teeth showing, then turned back to watch the movie.

When the movie got out, Jerry took us for a hot chocolate and we sat in the little café together, like a family. It was starting to weird me out. I wasn't used to this wholesome kind of behavior when it came to outings with Nini. Usually it was sex, drugs and rock and roll. This was like the Waltons or something. But Nini seemed to be enjoying it thoroughly, so I went with it. We talked briefly about Jerry's job, which was at a horse ranch. It was the first personal information either of us had heard about him, so we were curious. We learned that he took people on rides and cared for the horses. Nini hung on every word, concentrating on his face with a focus I was not familiar with. I wondered what she saw. What drew her to him? To me he was a cypher. He was only interesting in that he was so uninteresting, so unknown. He revealed almost nothing.

He watched, he smiled. Who was he? Did Nini know?

The drive home was cold. I couldn't really see into the cab as it was now dark, and there were no dash lights in the old truck. Bored, I tried desperately to light a cigarette. After a good 10 minutes of trying, the flint on my lighter wore out and I quit. I lay back in the bed and stared up at the stars. I thought about what they might be talking about in the cab. Was Nini asking him questions about the horse ranch? Was he asking her questions about school? What did they have in common? Why had he reacted strangely to her putting her hand on his leg? What was he after, if not that? As we approached the coast a thick layer of fog covered the sky, and my view of the stars disappeared.

"Jerry wants us to come to his house this weekend for a party," Nini said as we walked up to the house, the sound of his truck heading out of town still audible in the distance.

"He wants US to come?" I asked, genuinely confused. "What's his trip?"

"He likes you. His little sister is going to be there, he wants to introduce you to her. Thinks you guys would get along."

"Huh. OK. Sounds cool," I said as we entered the house.

The party was small, maybe 15 people. When we arrived Jerry was jamming on his bass with a couple of guys in their early 20s. They played a couple of Grateful Dead songs, then Jerry handed the bass off to another guy and he started barbecuing oysters on a little deck that hung out over the bay. Nini stepped out with him while I sat in the corner, trying to get an angle on the situation. Nini and I were the youngest there by far, except for a girl, maybe 15 years old, who I presumed was Jerry's sister. She was out in the little garden in front of the house, chatting with a couple of women in their 20s and what seemed like their husbands. Everyone was very nice, hippie-dippie, but I felt horribly self-conscious and out of place.

Finally, Jerry walked over to me.

"I want you to meet my sister. She lives in Mill Valley. She's about the same age as you, and she really likes skateboarders," he said as I got up and followed him out the front door and into the little garden.

"Vishna, have you guys met yet?" Jerry said as we stepped up to the girl. She was very pretty, with olive skin and a head of scrambled, curly hair. Big hoop earrings framed her face with an air of adulthood, but her ripped jeans and leather jacket reinforced her youth. She smiled at me.

"No, but I've been watching you," she said through her plump, smooth lips. She hadn't been, or at least I hadn't noticed her doing so.

Embarrassed, I just smiled. She moved closer to me. She smelled like roses.

"Do you drink? You want a beer?" she asked as she smiled into my face.

"Sure." I was overwhelmed by her presence, which seemed at once as ethereal as her scent and as crushing and visceral as her full breasts and muscular, athletic legs. My hands shook as she handed me a cold can of beer from a nearby cooler. She opened one herself and looked me over, then leaned into my ear.

"Your hands are shaking," she whispered with a sweet lilt in her voice, dragging the words across her lips almost as if she had a lisp. It was the sexiest thing I had ever encountered. My body began to shake as well. She sensed it. She put her hand on my chest and unbuttoned the top button of my shirt. I scanned the faces of the adults around us. No one seemed to give a shit.

"Breathe," she said, letting the "th" linger between her teeth for just a moment.

I swallowed, but I didn't breathe. I concentrated on my

hands and opened my beer. She clinked hers with mine and stepped back, spreading her fantastic lips across her large white teeth.

"Cheers."

"Cheers."

Vishna looked over my shoulder at the three middle-aged fishermen who were sharing a joint near the gate. She walked past me and joined them. I finally took a breath and looked around for Nini. I found her in the kitchen, preparing some oysters to barbecue. Jerry was showing her how to shuck them, working the small knife into the shell, then letting her twist and open it. I watched as the two of them laughed and chatted. Jerry aged her. She seemed so grown up. They sipped white wine from glasses with stems. Kids didn't laugh and chat as they shucked oysters. Kids didn't sip white wine. Not us, anyway. This was a new Nini. I felt distant from her. I could not laugh and chat. Or shuck oysters. She was among them, the adults. I was not. I was a visiting child. A virgin. But there was Vishna stepping in through the sliding glass door, her eyes newly glazed. She smiled at me …

The sun went down over the bay, and Jerry lit a fire in the little fireplace in the garden as Nini curled up in a chair with an old, drab army blanket around her. I stood on the small deck and watched the last of the sun's rays dance across the bay, silhouetting the opposite shore. I squinted my eyes, trying to make out Hearts Desire Beach, which I estimated to be directly across from us.

I imagined Bodi standing on the beach, his ankles breaking the tiny waves as they rolled in. I pictured him staring across the bay with an eagle's vision — staring through me, through the walls of Jerry's tiny house, into the garden where he could see Nini dreamily watching Jerry stoke the fire. Was he jealous of her new affection?

Did Bodi care? Had he ever cared? Or was he just looking for someone to suck his dick? Did Bodi see me? What did he see? Was I fooling anyone with the cigarettes, the beer? Bodi was just a kid, too. He was no man, not like Jerry. Jerry had killed a deer. He had a house. He hadn't tried to fuck Nini. Or get a blowjob. He treated her like a woman, even if she was just a girl. I imagined myself standing there with Bodi. Looking across the bay, back at myself. I saw a boy. My heart sank. I had never really thought of it before in such stark terms. I was not a man. I was a boy. Was Nini a woman? Did being treated as a woman make her one? Did I want to be a man? Would having sex make me one? Did Nini want to be a woman? We were kids …

Most of the guests had drifted back into the hills and only Nini, Jerry, Vishna and I remained, save for one of the fishermen, who had passed out on a pile of nets in the corner of the garden. The sun had gone down over the bay, Bodi had gone back where he came from and I had forgotten about the questions that had riddled me about my manhood.

I sat on a wicker loveseat across from Nini, who was still curled up in the blanket. Jerry sat on a eucalyptus stump by the fire, stoking it with a metal rod. Vishna walked out from the kitchen with two fresh beers. She handed me one as she sat down on the loveseat beside me.

"Getting cold," she said as she pulled the arms of her oversized sweater over her hands to shield them from the cold can of beer.

"You want a blanket, Vishna?" Jeff said to his sister in a fatherly way.

"Yeah. Should I get a couple?" Vishna asked as she disappeared into the house.

"Sure," Jerry nodded, as he turned his attention to Nini, smiling at her. "Don't go falling asleep on me …"

"I'm not. Just getting comfy," Nini smiled back. Her eye was drifting. Jerry correctly intuited this as a sign that she was getting sleepy.

Vishna returned with a couple more thick, wool army blankets and dropped one next to Jerry. He let it sit. She spread one over me, then sat down beneath it on her side of the loveseat. She smiled at me and slid her toes under my thigh. I looked over to Nini for backup, but she was asleep. She had drunk a considerable amount of wine that afternoon and had also risen early that morning to go jogging, something she had recently begun to do, after searching long and hard for a "sports bra" that would hold her giant boobs. She had been complaining a lot that she was "getting fat" and needed to exercise, but had used the lack of the sports bra for an excuse not to, complaining it hurt to have her tits bouncing around in her face. But now she had found one and had started running every morning. I was impressed with her dedication.

The rest of us sat there for a while, silently looking at the fire. The embers danced in Vishna's big brown eyes. Her toes tickled my thigh as she slowly moved each one in order, repeating with each foot — left foot, right foot, left foot, right foot. It was surprisingly erotic. Every so often she would turn and smile at me. A closed-mouth smile, not breaking over her teeth, but wide and friendly, and each time she smiled her eyes would narrow, leaving the impression of total focus ... on me. It felt good. Jerry sat there with a grin on his face, his top teeth showing slightly. For the first time he looked kind of dumb, sitting there with a grin on his face, silently watching the fire. I couldn't detect any thought from his expression, just a dumb stare and a dumb grin. Huh ... I didn't know what to think. This guy had seemed so sly, so in control. Was he really just a dummy, silently floating through life, catching flies as they landed in his open mouth?

Finally, Jerry looked away from the fire long enough to notice Vishna smiling at me, so he stood up and bent over Nini, lifting her easily in his arms, then carrying her inside, still with the vacant smile. Vishna and I watched him go, then she turned to me and smiled again. I grew uncomfortable as the smile lingered this time. She pushed her toes further under my thigh, until they were free to wiggle between my legs. Showtime. It was now or never. Do I make the first move? Hadn't she already made it with all the looks, smiles, toes?

"Breathe."

I realized I hadn't taken a breath since Jerry carried Nini away. I took a halting breath. Vishna leaned up so that her chin rested on her knees. She smiled again, this time showing her teeth. I took a deep breath and slid my hands around the backs of her calves. I pulled her in. She put her arms around my neck and brought her soft, full lips to mine. She was a good kisser. The kind of kisses that made it feel like you were kissing with your whole body. I felt her boobs. They were medium sized and firm in her bra. She put her hand on my crotch. I already had a boner, and she began to rub it, though the awkward angle she was at made it tricky.

THUMP. The fisherman who had fallen asleep on a pile of nets had rolled off and fallen onto the wooden deck. He grabbed his cap, looked around, saw us entangled and stumbled to the gate, disappearing through it. Vishna chuckled, then turned back to me and looked into my eyes. She began to kiss my neck. Down she moved, pulling up my shirt, ducking under the blanket. She began to unbuckle my pants. I sat erect, head above the covers, looking around the small garden area, keeping a close watch on the door to the house, terrified Jerry might come back out to check on us or the fire … . Vishna took my dick in her hand and started to stroke it, then quickly put it in her mouth and started to suck. I tensed up. She took it out and put a hand on my stomach.

"Breathe."

I took a deep breath. I was shaking. She held her hand to my stomach for a moment and began again. Damn. So this is what all the fuss is about, I thought. This feels fucking great. This is awesome. I watched the door. Oh shit. It's coming … . Vishna sped up, sensing I was nearly finished. It felt as if she took me completely into her mouth as I came. She swallowed, keeping me in her mouth until I finally took a breath and my body sighed to a calm. I finally took my eyes off the door and looked down as she slowly emerged from beneath the blanket.

Immediately I filled with regret. She smiled and put her head against my chest, but every fiber of my being burned to get up and away from her. I felt a biological warning going off inside of me, filling me with nausea. What was this? I hadn't expected it. Why was I feeling this way? I looked down at her beautiful face, but all I could see was a sister. Not Nini, not our younger sister, but a sister, my sister. I was disgusted with myself for letting her give me head. How could I have subjected her to this, when we were clearly not meant to be lovers? She felt like my fucking sister. She looked up at me and smiled.

"How was that?"

I tried to smile, but couldn't. She sat up and kissed me. I could taste the salty brine of my cum on her lips. That didn't help. I reflexively pulled back.

"Sorry," she said as she wiped her mouth, then reached for her beer, and took a sip, sloshing it around in her mouth for effect. She leaned in and kissed me again, but I pulled back again.

"What's wrong?"

"I know this is going to sound really weird, but … I feel like … I feel like you're my sister." All the lightness, the warmth, the comfort, left her face.

"What?"

"I know … I don't know … I just … I suddenly got this weird feeling."

"After you came in my mouth or before?"

She had a damn good point.

"After," I said, ashamed. "I'm sorry."

Not good enough. She was pissed. She shook her head, then got up and went inside, leaving me alone in the garden. I looked over to the fire — it was dying, and it was getting cold out. I pulled the blanket up over my chest, then reached down and pulled my pants up and buttoned them.

"You're such a dipshit," Nini said from behind her typewriter. She sat cross-legged on her overly high bed, surrounded by paper, with her antique portable typewriter set up in front of her. The Grateful Dead's "Shakedown Street" warbled out from her crappy boombox, which sat too close to the little potbelly stove near her bed.

"I know. I don't know what the fuck happened, but I was so into her, literally I was thinking as we kissed that she was going to be my girlfriend forever, I was like totally falling in love with her in that moment. Then she went down and I thought I was in fucking heaven. And she was so good at it."

"Did she hold it with one hand at the base and suck the end? Did she tickle your balls? Did she deep-throat you?" Nini asked, looking down at the poem she was working on. I guessed she was comparing technique.

"And then the second I came, I felt like a total weirdo and that she was like my sister," I said, ignoring her questions.

"I just had this really weird feeling. Like it was wrong. Like a physical feeling that we shouldn't be having sex."

"That's pretty weird." She looked up at me. "You don't have a weird sister-thing do you? Because I can tell you, I'm totally not into that," she said with an air of sophistication, as if she knew people who might be "into that." Then she laughed.

"Fuck no! I don't know what it was. And like half an hour later the feeling was totally gone, and I wished I could have just kept cool because I really like her."

"Yeah, not going to happen now. She's totally over it," Nini said as she began typing again. "Did this happen when Sasha gave you head?"

I hung my head and shook it "no." I looked up and could see that Nini knew I hadn't been completely honest about it.

"Weird that it only happened with Vishna," she said, smiling.

"Yeah. I … didn't come with Sasha. She just put it in her mouth for a second."

"I knew it. You would have been gushing if you'd come. Feels too good not to talk about."

"Did you and Jerry do it?" I asked, desperate to change the conversation.

She shook her head.

"I passed out."

"I know, but …"

"No, I woke up in his bed with all my clothes on. When he woke up we just talked until he made us breakfast."

"So what do you guys talk about?" I asked, changing gears.

"I don't know. Not much. His boat that he's fixing up. Camping. He loves camping."

"You really like him?"

"I don't know. I think so. I can't tell until I have sex with him, but he's going to Baja for two months … . Maybe we're just friends."

"Maybe they're weird …" I said, floating the idea. "She's like, a nympho, and he's a celibate."

"Maybe you're weird. In fact I know you're weird," she smiled. "At least you finally got your dick sucked, and came. Was that part fun at least?"

I thought back to it. Vishna's lips were so soft, her long curly hair had tickled my abdomen as she was down there. She had been so cool. I did really like her. I thought she was beautiful and smart. She didn't look like us, like a sister. What the fuck was wrong with me? Why had I felt so weird? Was I sister-gay? No, I had no interest in my sisters sexually. But something was amiss.

"It was awesome," I said.

Nini smiled and continued typing.

GLEN.

Nini put her seatbelt on and started the car. She shifted into gear, and the big blue Volvo wagon lurched down the hill towards town. As we passed the store we both looked around to see if anyone was hanging out, anyone that might see us driving. Driving ourselves. Only old Jim, a neighborhood octogenarian, was standing on the corner, his cap pulled down over his wrinkled eyes, his big worker hands shoved in his jeans. He watched us go by, but I doubt he thought we were cool — not as cool as we were feeling, anyway.

"Where'd you put those smokes?" I asked Nini.

"In my purse."

I reached into the back seat and pulled her purse onto my lap. I rifled through it, looking for the pack. I pulled out a beige disc made of plastic. It had little pills spread out in a circle packed in foil.

"What the fuck is this?" I asked, thinking perhaps it was some kind of drug she had neglected to share with me.

"My pills, dummy."

"Your pills? What kind of pills?"

"Birth control."

I stared at the disc.

"I have to take one every day. The blue ones are just sugar pills I take while I'm on my period so I don't get out of the habit."

I had never seen birth-control pills. Our mother had always left her diaphragm on the nightstand near her bed, so I knew what that was, but pills? No.

"Do they always work?"

"Supposedly."

I took her word for it and dug around until I found the cigarettes. I lit two and handed her one.

We wound down the bay road, past the Marshall Tavern, shuttered and lonely, past Jerry's little house, which was still unoccupied. We passed the old Synanon cult's ranch, and the Marshall store, a little shack that sold bait and crappy sandwiches. Nini drove slowly, relaxed behind the wheel. We both savored the ride and wondered how we might be perceived when we got to Point Reyes, 15 miles or so down the bay. It had been some time since we had ventured this far south, spending most of our free time with new friends from school. Now we had a car, and Nini was itching to show her independence and to prove to herself and others that she was over Rod. A car! No more hitching rides, no more begging for a place to crash. We were autonomous. Free. At least Nini was, and I could count on her. We had wheels. But no radio. It was broken, and my mother loved to sing in the car so had no intention of fixing it. We sang "Karma Chameleon," leaning our heads together not in harmony, but in out-of-phase unison, which created a strange, tin-can-sounding effect, especially on the "karma karma karma" part.

We moved on to "Let's Dance" and "Modern Love." We smoked incessantly, only waiting a few moments between each cigarette. I made a big deal about the cigarette lighter.

Only those with a car, and the ability to smoke in it, light their smokes with the convenience of a push-button lighter. My exaggerated use of it made Nini laugh. We kept the windows down, even though it was foggy and cold. The wind didn't affect the cigarette lighter, anyway. We took our time and enjoyed the ride, even while we champed at the bit of excitement that we both felt from being granted such freedom.

We pulled into Point Reyes and parked in front of the bakery just as it began to grow dark. The bakery's lights glowed a warm amber, diffused by the thick fog. We watched as the middle-aged lady who ran the place packed it up for the night. This was usually a key meeting point in town, especially on a Friday night. But tonight it was dead. We'd been so distracted by the sheer delight of having our own transportation that we hadn't bothered, as Nini usually did, to set anything up. We were just showing up, hoping to happen upon a party, which Friday night usually provided. But not tonight.

We sat on the curb and smoked. The lady from the bakery locked up and disappeared into the night.

"This sucks," I finally admitted.

"Maybe we should go to Olema, see if Mona is around."

My heart jumped.

"Isn't she going out with Tony Marchese?"

"Yep. But maybe her mom's out of town, maybe they're having a party."

My heart sank. Tony was 19, and his dad let him drive his blue Porsche speedster. He was short but had a body like a gymnast and always had his shirt off. Mona was completely out of range now.

"I don't know. Let's hang out here for a few more minutes, see if anybody shows up." Neither of us said his name, but Rod was on both our minds. Nini was eager to show him she no longer cared but equally terrified that she might not be able to prove it once she saw him.

"What's up, Nini?" a voice called out from the darkened park, a few yards from where we sat on the high curb. A cigarette ember glowed in the dark, then sparked as it was flicked against a tree. The voice was slow and deep, with what almost sounded like a Southern drawl. What cowboy lurked in the darkness there? What man was watching us from the shadows? No man. A boy. Glen Whatley stepped out of the darkness and walked towards us.

"Haven't seen you in a while." Glen poured the words out like thick gravy. He was tall and lanky, with long, stringy blond hair. His jean jacket hung from his shoulders as if on a hanger, and his jeans dragged behind his old tennis shoes, straggling in the dirt. His long, droopy face was friendly, and his eyes twinkled, even in the foggy night. Glen and I were the same age. His older brother, Chris, had had a thing for Nini for years, but she saw him strictly as a friend. This was pretty rare, for Nini to put someone so squarely in the friend zone, but Chris was in it and he wasn't getting out. It really bugged him, and he showed off for Nini a lot, trying in vain to impress her into liking him.

Glen didn't give a fuck who liked him. He liked everyone, but his affection came with no condition. He was just a friendly kid. He passed me and sat down next to Nini.

"Hey Glen. Where is everyone?" Nini said, cheerily.

"I don't know," he replied, slowly shaking his head in agreement with himself. "I think there's a big party somewhere, but Chris split before I could ask him where it is. What are you guys doing, just came to town to look for excitement?" This struck me as kind of a funny way to ask the question, but he was so nice …

"I'm here, though. You guys want to party with me?" He said slowly, then threw his head back and laughed a deep, throaty laugh. Once he had stopped laughing he looked at us, grinning generously.

"You have no idea where the party is?" Nini asked, sounding a little desperate. Perhaps the idea of spending our Friday night "partying" with Glen had scared her.

He shook his head.

"Hearts Desire? Mt. Vision? Drakes Beach?" Nini said, rattling off all the usual party spots.

"No idea. Could be any of those places. If we had a car we could drive around and look, but even then …"

"Dude, we have a car," I blurted out.

Glen sat in the front so he could help with directions, as we were going to try some places even Nini wouldn't have found on her own. The fog darkened the night, and the narrow roads out to the coast wound back and forth dangerously. I sat leaning forward between the two seats, the three of us dimly lit by the dashboard lights.

We drove up Mt. Vision, to the parking lot where everyone usually gathered. Only a couple of beer bottles sat haphazardly on the asphalt. Had they been here? Glen got out to look around for clues.

I thought of the last time we had been here, when Nini had made such a fool of herself. I looked at her and could tell she was thinking the same thing, gazing around, trying to piece the night together with the vague recollections she had. It had taken her a long time to get over the shame of that night, so I didn't bring it up.

"Nope. I don't think they were up here. Those bottles look like they've been sitting there for a couple days. Got bugs in 'em and stuff," Glen reported as he climbed back into the car. Nini gave Glen the once-over. Had his detective skills just inspired Nini to suddenly view Glen as a possible hook-up? We drove on.

The road to Drakes Beach was slammed in with fog,

and we could only drive 10 miles an hour most of the way there, with Nini and Glen both leaning into the windshield to try and see through the dense, swirling gray soup. This caused the window to fog up, and Glen wiped it constantly with his sleeve. When we finally got to the parking lot, it was deserted. No fires raged on the beach. No drunk girls wandering into the dark to pee. It was dark, and it was getting late.

Glen walked to the edge of the sand and looked out at the crashing waves, only just visibly lit by the Volvo's headlights.

"Maybe everybody went to Mona's party," Glen lamented. Nini and I looked at each other. It was at least an hour to Mona's house in Olema from here, in the fog.

"Mona's having a party? Why didn't you tell us when we were in town?" I asked Glen.

"I guess I should have," Gene drawled back at me, still watching the waves. "But then we would have missed this."

"Missed what?" I asked, looking to Nini, who smiled and looked back at Glen, obviously admiring him.

"Being right here, right now."

"Fuck," I said as I turned away.

I climbed back into the car. I sat in the back seat and watched Nini step over to Glen. They talked and laughed, agreeing on something. They walked back to the car.

"We're going to go to Glen's house," Nini said as she started the car.

"Why?"

Glen turned back to me. "Because I've got a big joint there," he said, smiling a wide, toothy smile that — just for a moment — made his face less droopy, but no less funny-looking.

I didn't smoke weed, so this was a non-starter for me. Nini didn't really either, but partying was neither here nor there for her at this point. She'd set her sights on Glen.

"I'm sorry I withheld information," Glen said without looking back at me. "I just really didn't want to go to Mona's because my brother is being a dick. And I've totally been wanting to hang with you." Now he looked at Nini and they smiled at each other.

Glen lived with his parents in an old, weatherbeaten wooden house, right near the bakery in Point Reyes. His room was on the opposite side of the house from his sleeping parents' room, so noise wasn't a big issue. We settled into a little sitting area around an old bass drum-turned coffee table, and Glen lit the joint. His room was cluttered, but clean. A drum set dominated, but there was room for a double bed, the little sitting area and a mountain bike, which hung by its tires from hooks in the ceiling. A photo of John Coltrane, ripped from a magazine, was pinned to the wall above the bed.

Glen took a big hit, then passed it to Nini, who took a modest hit and offered it to me, knowing full well I'd refuse. I hadn't smoked pot since a terrifying fear of werewolves had begun to grip me after even the smallest hit. Nini handed the joint back to Glen, who took another big hit, then set it in an ashtray full of roaches.

"Your parents are cool with all the roaches lying around?" Nini asked, her eye drifting west.

Glen smiled another wide one. "Where do you think I got the J? They're cool. Chris totally bakes with them, but I kinda just snag one here and there. Smoke by myself or with my friends."

I couldn't get over his voice. It was so deep. Skinny guys often had that deep voice. Nini and I had even once discussed this phenomenon, and Glen in particular. She had suggested that it also meant they had big dicks, but she had never been with a guy with a voice like that, so couldn't prove it. Perhaps that's what she intended to do tonight …

"Got anything to drink?" I asked, expecting water.

"There's a bottle of white wine behind your chair, but it's like a week old."

I leaned back over the little ratty upholstered chair I was sitting in and found the half-empty bottle, its cork long since missing. I smelled it. It didn't smell good, but it didn't smell rotten. I took a little swig. Nini and Glen watched me, waiting for a reaction. I shrugged.

"It's not bad," I lied and offered them some. They both shook their heads. I shrugged again and took a bigger swig.

"You play drums?" I asked, motioning to the kit, as if he might not understand otherwise.

"Yup."

Nini looked at me long. I knew what it meant. She was ready to make a move, and I was getting in the way. I took the bottle and walked to the door, which led to a little porch on the driveway.

"I'm gonna have a look around outside, see what there is to see." I stepped out onto the porch as they watched me go.

"Watch out for the fuzz with that bottle. Nick the Prick is probably prowling tonight," Glen said over his shoulder, then turned back to Nini as I shut the door. She and I exchanged one last nod and a glance which I knew meant to stay out a while, but not too long. By now I was pretty familiar with how long it would take.

I walked down the driveway and out onto the darkened street, past the little park where we had found Glen. The town was dead. Not a soul. I could see down the street that the Western bar was still open, but no one was standing outside, and it was quiet and still. Fog swirled in the air, but it was thin and low, and I could see stars if I looked straight up. I took a swig, then held the bottle close to my leg to hide it should a car come, and strolled down Main Street past the dark shops and restaurants. There weren't many. Main Street was maybe 300 yards long. I walked past the feed store and hopped up onto a bale of hay, then sat down on it and killed the bottle. Just as I leaned back to stash the bottle behind the bale, headlights broke the night and I stiffened up, trying to slowly bring my hand back up without being noticed.

The County Sheriff's Bronco pulled up to within five feet of me and stopped, its headlights bright in my eyes. Nick the Prick got out and slowly walked up to me, his hand on his gun. I stayed seated and smiled. Nick was young for a sheriff's deputy, maybe 24, and he had a chip on his shoulder, hence the nickname. I had only had minor interactions with him, mostly bullshit like flicking a cigarette butt or spitting on the sidewalk. Nick never remembered me, which was a good thing, as it prevented my minor infractions from building up into a bigger one. I always got to start from zero.

"Hi."

"Whatcha up to?"

"Just taking a little walk. My sister's hanging out with a boyfriend and she needed some privacy. So I'm giving them an hour or so to take care of business." I felt good about this explanation, and capped it with a smile.

"Oh yeah, who's your sister?"

"Her name's Nini."

He thought for a moment. His stance shifted, and he suddenly became far less intimidating.

"She the little blonde girl with the …?" He held his cupped hands up to his chest. "… wandering eye?"

Oh. So he was watching her. Carefully. Noticing her big tits was a given, but most people didn't notice Nini's eye until they knew her pretty well or had been watching her for a while, sizing her up.

"Yes. She does have a sleepy eye. I don't know if I'd call it wandering …" I said, trying to imply that her wanderings may not extend to him.

"Who's her boyfriend?"

"I said a boyfriend. He's not her boyfriend."

"Don't be a shit. Who's she with?"

"Kid named Glen."

"Glen Whatley? He's 14 years old."

I shrugged. "She's only 17." I meant it. What the fuck did he care?

Nick looked over towards Glen's house, deciding his next move. He started pacing, getting a little hot.

"That little fucker is always pulling shit."

I wondered how hanging out with Nini was "pulling shit."

Nick paced around a little too far and spotted the bottle, stashed behind the hay bale.

"Oh. Here we go."

He picked up the bottle and looked at me.

"White-wine drinker, huh?"

"That's not mine."

"Uh huh. Well let's see what the breathalyzer thinks …" He walked over to his truck.

Shit. I thought about running, but he'd just catch me and I'd really be fucked.

He popped the case and pulled out the tube. The radio crackled.

"Hey Nick, you in town still?" a woman's voice asked. She sounded strained and familiar.

He picked up the mic.

"Yeah, what's up?" he spat back.

"We got a report of a collision on Hwy 1, two miles north of Olema. Must be right outside of town. Sounds pretty bad. Fire department is on the scene."

Nick looked at me dismissively and tossed the tube back in its case. He jumped in the Bronco without another word and sped off.

I watched him go, then followed him, down Main Street towards the south edge of town where the buildings abruptly stopped along with the town. As I passed the Western bar I could see, through the window, that it was a slow night. A couple of locals were at the bar, and one fucked-up-looking middle-aged lady was dancing by herself on the dance floor to some shitty country song. I rounded the corner by the deli and I could see the flashing lights about a quarter-mile south of town. The fire department was there, as was Nick's Bronco. Two cars were smashed into each other, head on. I hopped a fence and continued towards the wreck, walking in the grass, parallel to the road.

When I got about a hundred yards away I could make out what kind of cars they had been. An orange Plymouth Roadrunner and a Dodge van. Bodi. Bodi's Roadrunner. I didn't recognize the van. Nick and a couple of firemen were standing around, talking on the radio. There seemed to be no sense of urgency. An ambulance approached from the south. When it arrived, two paramedics jumped out, but after speaking with the others, they just looked inside the cars and shook their heads. I walked back to town.

I quietly knocked on the door. Glen's deep voice responded.

"Give us 10 more minutes."

I turned and walked back to the street and sat on the curb. I was out of cigarettes, so I laid back and looked up at the stars. Damn. Bodi was dead. That was crazy. I thought back to the times I had been in his car, careening down the winding roads of the bay. How many times had Nini been in his car, no seatbelt, giving him head as he drove down some foggy lane. I wondered if there was anyone with him. Who was driving the van? Who's fault had it been? I imagined he was coming from Mona's party, just two miles from where he had met his end. What had the party been like? I imagined it as a dimly lit affair, Mona sitting on Tony's lap, laughing and swaying as Led Zeppelin or Van Morrison played on the stereo. I imagined Rod standing in the kitchen, leaning against the counter, arms folded, bored. No available girls, perhaps. Maybe he had decided to head home rather than slog through a night with no hook-up. Or maybe he had a girl in the car with him. Some girl like Nini, who he was driving out to some lonely place. A place where she would give him head. Or perhaps even the girl that had diverted his attention from Nini — surely there was one? No one would give up such a cushy situation without another waiting in the wings.

I guessed it had been 10 minutes, so I walked back to the door and knocked again. Glen's deep voice answered again.

"Come on in."

I opened the door and walked in. Nini was tying her shoes. Glen was dismantling a couple of roaches to roll into a new joint.

"Where'd you go?" Nini asked.

"Walked around, almost got busted by Nick the Prick, but he got a call about a car crash." Nini and Glen both looked at me. They braced for it.

"I walked down about half a mile south of town to get a look," I said as my throat tightened. They both waited, motionless. I looked at Nini, and tears began to well in my eyes. She saw them, and tears welled in hers as well.

"Who was it?" she asked. I stalled.

"Who was it?" she asked again, fear rising in her voice.

"Come on, man," Glen joined in.

"Bodi."

Both of them leaned back as if hit by a cannonball, then slowly leaned forward in unison as if they were going to puke. Glen finally got the breath to speak.

"Are you sure it was him?"

"Orange Roadrunner, heading north from Olema, probably from Mona's house." Nini began to sob. She fell back onto Glen's bed and cried. I sat down and took a long breath, trying not to cry. Glen watched Nini cry. He had a strange look on his face, and as he studied her I wondered if he was jealous of her tears for another. After a little while Nini sat up.

"Bodi. Why Bodi?" she said, licking at the salty tears that kept falling. "I loved him."

Gene and I sat silently, unsure of how to respond.

Finally, I thought of something to say.

"He was cool."

The others nodded. I looked at Glen, who seemed to be reeling from Nini's admission of love. He was 14. Had he ever been in love? Was he in love with Nini? He moved over and sat next to Nini, putting his arm around her. Her head dropped onto his shoulder, and she continued crying. I noted his mature response.

The next morning the three of us walked over to the bakery, where a small crowd was gathered outside. The fog was thick, and it lent an ethereal vibe to the somber scene. Glen's brother, Chris, was there, along with a half-dozen other local kids.

"You hear about Bodi's car?" Chris asked as we walked up, eager to be the first to spread the news.

"He saw it," Glen said, motioning to me. I nodded.

"Was it gnarly?" a surfer-looking kid I didn't know asked. I nodded again.

"It was like the cars had melted into each other. They must have been hauling ass. When the paramedics got there they looked inside the cars and just shook their heads and stood around. Everyone must have been dead already." Nini winced.

"I bet Bodi is freaking about his car," the surfer kid said.

"I doubt he's worried about his car," another kid said.

Nini and I looked at each other.

"Who was driving the van? Did you see? Did they live?" Chris asked me.

"I didn't see."

"Did you see Troy?"

"Troy?"

"Yeah, he was driving Bodi's car. I doubt Bodi is worrying about his car when his best friend just bit the dust."

Nini's face went white. She moved to the fore, past Glen and me.

"Troy was driving? Was Rod in the car?" Nini pleaded.

"No, Rod was at Mona's. Troy took his car to go on a beer run."

"So Rod's alive?"

"Yeah. But Troy's dead."

Nini stepped back. All three of us took a breath.

"I thought you were there, dude?" Chris asked, with an accusatory tone. I ignored his question and looked at Nini, whose expression was changing rapidly. Troy was her friend. The grief of losing her friend was washing over her, but the relief of hearing that Rod was alive was overwhelming, and I could tell she was fighting off a smile. Awkwardly, Glen put his arm around Nini. Everyone stared. Chris shook his head in defeat. Glen just stood there, holding his ground. Nini didn't seem to mind. She wasn't even there any more, she was off with Rod, thundering down the road in his Roadrunner.

"So ... deep voice ... big dick," Nini said out of nowhere, with none of the levity that would usually accompany such a declaration. She slowed down for another hairpin turn, then looked at me. It was late morning, and we were heading north on Hwy 1, along the bay. We had left Glen and the others standing around at the bakery. Nini had kissed Glen goodbye in front of everyone, and this had left him visibly pumped.

"But he doesn't know how to use it," she continued. I imagined Glen deflating.

I nodded and looked away. Neither did I. At least he had a big dick. My dick was just normal sized, and I didn't know how to use it, either. I let the moment pass. The silence was pregnant with thoughts of Troy. Finally, as if acquiescing to an unspoken law that the dead must be lamented, Nini spoke.

"He had the nicest smile. I know that's super cheesy to say, but he did. He had those kind of goofy big lips, and he was usually smiling, but it was always nice. He was so nice. I wonder who he loved ..." I thought about this last question. Of course she wondered that. She loved Rod. But he didn't love her. He let her give him head, but it wasn't leading to love. She wanted him to love her, but knew he never would. She knew what it was not to be loved. Who had Troy loved? Who had loved him?

"He was always cool to me," I replied, unable to think of anything more profound to say. After a moment I continued. "I wonder who was driving the van ... ?" We sat in silence and contemplated this as Nini swung the car into another curve, then another, then another.

SANTO.

I sat down on his bed, and he was like 'Girls aren't allowed to sit on my bed.' I asked why, and he said because he can't stand a girl sitting on his bed without having sex with her," Nini recalled, while laying back on her bed. The light from the little bus's windows was soft, and she looked good, lying there naked.

I held the camera up to my face as she put an arm behind her head in what I imagined she thought was a very sexy pose. It *was* kind of sexy.

"And what did you say?"

"I said, 'OK.'"

Santo was a tall, good-looking guy with light-brown skin and Sid Vicious black hair. He wore a leather jacket with "The Damned" spray painted on the back. He also had a wandering eye. Unlike Nini's, his was always wandering. It was very difficult to know when he was looking at you, and this gave him an aloof quality, as if he could look at you and not look at you at the same time and it was no skin off his back either way. He lived with his mostly absent mother in an old Craftsman house in Santa Rosa. Santa Rosa had recently joined our sphere of reference when Nini got a job at the Hot Dog on a Stick at the mall, and we regarded it with excited caution. It was a bigger "town" than Petaluma and had a dangerous air about it. Somebody could get hurt there.

"So?"

"He's super good in bed. We had sex for like two hours."

"Probably 'cause he's on speed all the time," I said, having witnessed him popping cross tops like they were Tic Tacs.

"Whatever. He's like a jackhammer."

I clicked a shot, then lowered the camera.

"Is that like … do you actually like that? When a guy just … bam bam bam?"

Nini thought for a moment. I could tell that she hadn't really thought about whether she liked it or not.

"At the end. If a guy just does that from the beginning it's lame, but if he builds up to it, then yeah, that's how I can have an orgasm."

I was stunned. I had never heard her mention an orgasm. Not hers, anyway. She always talked about guys coming, but she'd never mentioned that she was having orgasms.

"Did you have an orgasm with Santo?"

She nodded. "He made me come twice."

"So girls come, too?" I asked, confused by the nomenclature.

"Of course. But they don't 'cum' come. Like, all over the place. We don't have cum. But we come."

I just stared at her.

"It's the same thing as an orgasm. Guys have orgasms and so do girls. Get it? And that's called coming for both."

I got it.

"I thought Santo had a girlfriend? That girl Monica. Isn't he going out with her?"

Nini sighed.

"Yeah, and I really like her, too."

"He probably cheats on her all the time."

"Yeah. She's so young, too. She has no idea."

She was my age, I think. She was cute. I had seen them making out in "Anarchy Alley," a breezeway off the main drag that the local punks hung out in, last time I was in Santa Rosa. She was too young for him, I had thought. Why do all the girls my age go for guys his age? Because they know how to fuck, I guessed.

"Did you hear about Nazi Mike?" Nini asked, assuming I knew who she was talking about. We'd only hung out in Santa Rosa a few times, and there were lots of kids there.

"What about him?" I knew who he was. I even liked him. I didn't believe he was a Nazi, even though he said he was, and wore the skinhead uniform of Levi's, Doc Martens, suspenders worn at the thigh and a green flight jacket. He was just a dumb, mixed-up kid that hung out in Anarchy Alley and fronted like everyone else, trying to fit in somewhere. He was goofy. He made everyone laugh.

"He got murdered."

I missed a breath.

"What?"

"Execution style. They found him out on Piner Road. Shot in the back of the head. I guess he was selling acid or something. A drug deal gone bad."

"Fuck. Do they know who did it.?"

"Well, you know that weird guy called Gory who hangs out sometimes? Kind of Goth?"

I didn't, but I nodded anyway.

"Well, I guess he disappeared, and people have been saying he had been hanging out a bunch with Mike, which is weird because he hated him and said so all the time."

"That's so fucked up. Mike was funny. I don't think he was a real Nazi."

"Nobody does."

"I hope they catch that guy."

I sat down on the chair by the potbelly stove. We were silent for a moment. Murder. MURDER.

"You want me to take any more?" I asked, holding the little Instamatic camera up.

"Take one where I'm on all fours, so you can really see how big my tits are."

"Do I have to?" I was surprised by Nini's cavalier attitude in the midst of such horrifying news.

I noticed her eyes had welled up with tears.

"Just one more."

BLAKE.

Eat out more often. Nini smiled and flashed the match book and it's maxim at me, then put it in her pocket as we stepped out of the crappy Chinese food restaurant onto Petaluma Boulevard. She got a big kick out of it and pulled it out of her pocket again just to read it to me.

"Eat out more often."

I'd recently started digging ditches for a family friend on his work sites and had a little cash to spread around. Nini was still working at Hot Dog on a Stick, wearing the stupid costume and pumping the lemonade. Guys would stop and just watch her and laugh; up and down, up and down … . So we could both afford to eat out once in a while. But lunch wasn't what was making her smile. Nini had recently discovered the virtues of cunnilingus and was thrilled that she'd found a boy who seemed to like doing it as much as she liked getting it. Blake lived in town, on Petaluma's suburban East Side, with his mom and his little brother. They were Irish Catholics and his mom was pretty into it, but Blake was a skate punk, like me. For once it was I who introduced Nini to someone, and she had become smitten immediately. Blake was a nice guy. He had a warm, delicate smile, reddish hair and a lean, strong body. He wasn't much of a skater, but Nini was hardly concerned with that. They had gotten together for the first time at the Friday night library skate sessions, where hordes of adolescent boys skated and drank cheap beer, and hordes of adolescent girls watched and drank wine coolers. Nini was somewhere in between. She was no ordinary skater Betty. She was one of the boys. They treated her differently, even though they wanted to fuck her like they wanted to fuck all the other girls. Somehow she was just different. She and Blake had gotten down to it in the back of the blue Volvo, right in the parking lot. Nini had given him head, and he had surprised her by going down on her right after.

"Let's go down to the plaza and see if Van the Man is around. Maybe he'll buy us some beer," Nini said as she walked and I rolled toward downtown. It was a late Saturday afternoon, and there would surely be some punks hanging out in front of the movie theater, cooking up a plan for the night.

"Hey, Van!" Nini said with a smile. Her eye was leaning pretty far out west. It always seemed to drift more when we were in town, but I could never figure out why.

"Hey, Nini. What's happening?" Van replied, returning the smile. He was a friendly dude in his early 20s. He was more of a hippie-holdover than a punk, with long, stringy black hair always pushed back in a red bandana. He wore an old army jacket, jeans and Chuck Taylors. He hung around in the little park in the middle of the boulevard across from the theater, when he wasn't working the projectors or taking tickets at the door. He was usually good for a 40-ouncer or two.

"Could you buy up for us?" Nini asked, bluntly.

Van chuckled self-consciously as if she had asked him for

a kiss. He was kind of awkward that way. Maybe that's why he didn't mind buying us beer. He wanted to be liked.

"What are you drinking?"

"Two Mickey's 40-ouncers."

"And a pack of Camels," I added.

We sat down on the park bench and waited. Dale Dork and Billie rolled up on their skateboards, both out of breath. I heard them before I saw them, and the sound of their wheels on the concrete made my heart race. Skateboarding had become a major preoccupation rather than just a hobby, and getting a chance to skate with some of the best from town was crazy exciting.

Dale and Billie sat down on the bench across from us. They both had closely shaven hair, Billie's with large, bleached-out dots all over. Dale took a quick hit off his inhaler. They didn't know me, but I knew them. I had watched them skate many times, too insecure to approach them.

"What's up, Nini?" Billie asked, his mouth forming the slightest of shy smiles. Billie was a god among the skate-punk crowd. He could *skate*. We all rolled around, but he could fly. He was like Baryshnikov on a skateboard, his arms and legs moving smoothly, in perfect concert. He was an artist. I was jealous that he had asked her and not me; I had the skateboard, after all, but then he probably didn't know my name. I could see by the way he looked at her that he really liked her. Everyone looked at her that way. Even the ones she didn't sleep with. I could see in Billie's face that he admired her. He was drawn to her. She somehow let them know, without saying or doing anything, that she was going to be nice. She wasn't going to judge. No matter what. It just wasn't in her.

"Hey, Billie. What's up?"

"Nothing. We just got chased by some cops for bombing

English Hill and running all the stop signs."

Dale Dork was giving me the once-over. He was a big guy, friendly, if a little suspicious. He looked over my board, my jean jacket, checking the "Dead Kennedys" button on my lapel. He must have approved, because he spoke to me, not to Nini.

"We're gonna go skate the humps, you wanna come?" he asked, his voice husky and optimistic.

"Sure. We're waiting for some beer."

Van came back a few minutes later and delivered our two big green bottles before disappearing into the theater. We walked a couple of blocks to an old car dealership, behind which were some concrete embankments. Nini watched from a curb, smoking and drinking her 40-ouncer as the three of us skated. After a 20-minute session, we all sat down and I proudly shared my beer with Billie and Dale. Dale was giving Nini the once-over now ...

"Can I have a sip of your beer?" Dale asked Nini, with surprisingly obvious overtones. She reached her arm out, and he put his hand on the bottle, both of them holding it at the same time for just a little too long. Interesting, I thought. The plan was to deliver the nude photos we'd taken to Blake. Nini had developed a real crush on him and was going to use the photos to seal the deal. But Dale was cool. He wasn't particularly handsome, but he had charisma — and reportedly a huge dick — thus the name Dale "Dork," dork being the "technical" term for a whale's penis.

Nini and Dale passed the bottle back and forth, and Billie and I did the same. My pleasure from sharing with Billie probably exceeded the anticipatory elation Nini and Dale were sharing. Billie was it. There was nothing better or cooler than him. And he and I were skating together and sharing a beer.

"There's a show at Mike's warehouse, you guys going?" Billie asked.

I looked at Nini.

"Rad. Yeah, we're going. You guys?"

They both nodded, but something had caught Dale's eye. A Petaluma PD cruiser had turned the corner and was headed for us.

"Cops!" Dale blurted out, chucking the nearly empty 40-ouncer into the gutter. We all jumped up and scattered. Billie ran through the garage of the car lot and I instinctively followed, running as fast as I could, beer in one hand, skate in the other. Billie was fast but he turned and looked back, slowing enough for me to follow. We came out the other side, onto Petaluma Boulevard, and ran up E Street towards the post office, finally stopping behind the old Carnegie Library. Billie and I waited breathlessly for the cops to catch up, but we had ditched them. All clear.

"You ever skate the junior high? There's some cool drops and banks and shit," Billie said, seeming to have forgotten Dale and Nini. I passed him the beer, and he took a long swig.

"I don't think so," I replied, not believing how awesome this day was turning out. "You think Nini and Dale got busted?"

"No way they caught Dale. Maybe Nini. But I bet they let her go. She wasn't doing anything. Dale had the beer," he said as he handed the bottle back to me. Here we were just sharing a beer and hanging out. Like friends.

I nodded in agreement as I killed the beer and tossed the bottle in some bushes, then followed Billie as he pushed off and rolled towards the junior high.

"The cop let me go. Dale ran down to the river and disappeared."

Nini was leaning against the brick wall of Mike's

warehouse with a few other punks, sharing a big can of Foster's Lager. The place was an old wood shop under a Mexican restaurant near the river. Mike and his buddy Goose made skateboards there, and on weekends bands played.

"He ditched you?" a girl with bleach-blonde hair and razor-blade earrings asked.

"No. We scattered, and I was the one the cops came after. I guess they knew I was the slowest. But they just asked me who the other kids were and asked me how old I was. I told them all I knew was your names were Tom and Jerry. They didn't seem to get it."

A band kicked off a song inside, and the other kids got up to go in, leaving Nini and me alone. She handed me the beer.

"So what did you do the rest of the day?" I asked. It had been four or five hours since we parted. I had gleefully spent the day skating with Billie. He'd shown me all his favorite spots and had even shown me a couple of tricks. I was in love.

"After the cops left I walked back over to Center Park. A few minutes later Dale came back. He got Van to buy us another 40, because he had thrown mine. He was paranoid, so we climbed up on the roof of the bookstore in the alley." She paused. I waited, anticipating some gory details.

"And …"

"It's true."

"What?"

"The dork part."

"That he has a whale dick?"

"Yeah."

"What is it about big dicks, anyway? How come everybody has such a big dick? I mean, does it really make a difference anyway? Is it that big of a deal?"

Nini thought for a moment.

"Well … not really… and not everybody has a big dick. I've been with … three guys with big dicks? It's … it's kind of exciting. Like … big tits? Do they make sex better? I doubt it. But it's exciting, right? You know?"

I did not.

"If a guy has a big dick, it's a turn-on. You're kind of like … OK … I have to deal with this big fucking dick! If I'm gonna give him head, it's a commitment, and I'm gonna have to really work hard. And if we have sex it's gonna hurt a little. But it's like … 'Oh! He has a big dick, cool.' But I guess for the most part it's not really a big deal. Better than a tiny dick!"

I nodded, taking it all in.

"So you guys fucked? On the roof?"

"Yeah. I wasn't going to … because …"

"Blake?"

"Yeah. But we finished the 40 and we were talking and … this sounds funny because Dale is such a … dork! I mean he acts like a total dork."

It was true. He behaved like a clown, often skating in just his underwear, exchanging loogies with his buddies … teenage dork stuff. But he always made it seem cool. This had made his name confusing, though. Was he Dale Dork because he was a dork, or because he had a dork? I guess it was both.

"He's really… sensitive. He likes poetry. I read him my new poem. He actually knew what it was about… and it's pretty abstract. He totally got it. Of course, right in the middle of it he asked if he could jiggle my tits. Such a dork!"

"And you let him, I'm guessing?"

She nodded, took the beer back and took a swig.

"I told him he could jiggle my boobs if he'd listen to another poem."

Fair deal, I thought.

"So he put his hands on my boobs but he didn't jiggle them, he just like, rubbed them gently. And it was really sexy. He played with my nipples. So instead of reading another longer poem, I recited my poem 'Wings' to him, you know that one?"

"Yeah. It's super short, it's like a couple of lines."

"Well, I was getting super horny from him rubbing my boobs. So I recited 'Wings' really fast, then we started kissing. The roof is made of this tar paper kind of stuff and it's really rough, I bet my butt looks like a raspberry."

I thought back to Sasha on the roof of school. Why had I chickened out? Why was I scared to try? Failure. I was sure I'd make a fool of myself. But wasn't I making a fool of myself anyway? Things had gone pretty well when Vishna gave me head, aside from my weird sister thing. Surely I'd figure out how to do it … . I decided I wouldn't chicken out again. Next time I got the chance, I was taking it. No matter what.

"And he has a huge dick," I lamented.

"Not as big as Marcus's. But big." She put the beer down and held her hands out about eight inches apart. I snatched the beer and drained it.

"So what about Blake?"

"Normal sized."

"No, what about him? I thought you liked him."

"Well, don't tell him."

"Are you still going to show him the pictures?"

"Yeah! It's not like we're going out yet. I didn't cheat on him."

"Is he here?"

"I haven't seen him.

"Did you call him?"

She shook her head. I could see that she felt a little guilty.

Not too much, but a little.

We went inside and watched the band — some punks from San Francisco. I liked it. Nini was over it. Not the people, just the music. She was now mostly listening to "hippie" music — the Grateful Dead, Van Morrison and her favorite, Loudon Wainwright III.

Dale and Billie were skanking with a few other kids. Dale gave Nini the occasional smile as he worked his way around the little mosh pit. I was impressed he wasn't ignoring her. Hit-and-run on a roof seemed like a recipe for never talking again, to me. I had still not even looked at Sasha since our roof episode, but Dale was cooler than me so of course he didn't do it how I thought I would probably do it. Soon I noticed that he was smiling his goofy smile at all the girls. Nini noticed, too. He got behind a particularly pretty girl and started to dry hump her leg. She pushed him off, then laughed. He started to do it again and this time she only laughed, she didn't push him off. Nini didn't seem to mind; in fact she laughed, too, and I could tell it was a relief. Someone else had caught her eye, and she was losing interest in Dale fast. Across the room a curly haired kid with dazzling blue eyes was staring at Nini. She kept looking over at him, then to Dale, then around the room, then back, but he just stared at her. His name was Logan. I had seen him around, skating and hanging out with some of the older punks. He asked the guy next to him a question I couldn't hear over the loud music and gestured towards Nini. He heard the answer and nodded, then resumed staring. Nini and I shared a look — how come he keeps staring? Nini smiled.

"Who is that?" Nini asked, shouting in my ear.

"I think his name is Logan. He's friends with Billie's older brother Chas."

"I saw him in front of the theater today, after we split up.

He was staring at me. Is he a weirdo?" she asked.

"I don't know. He seems OK."

She nodded as we watched a short blonde girl, not unlike Nini in her short and curvy stature, come up and take his hand. He looked uncomfortable as he tried to stop staring, but couldn't keep his eyes off of Nini. She didn't turn away, returning his gaze. His girlfriend finally noticed and pulled him in for a kiss. Nini turned away and moved to the back of the room.

I spotted Santo near the door, chatting real close with a tall girl whose name I didn't know. She had the sides of her head shaved and wore heavy purple eye makeup. I wondered where Monica might be. Moments later I found out. She was huddled in a pile on the other side of the room, her face awash with tears. Nini had already found her and was crouched down beside her, comforting her. It was too loud to hear what they were saying, but it was pretty clear it involved Santo. Nini pulled her up and they walked over to me. She shouted in my ear.

"Let's go. I want to drop the pictures off."

"Really? Tonight? That seems… I don't know …"

The band finished their song.

"I'm not going to go in. I'm going to put the envelope in his mailbox."

"You better hope his mom doesn't open it."

"That would be really funny," she said as Monica and I exchanged glances.

"Monica is coming with us."

Holy shit. I nodded and looked over to the door where Santo was. I wondered if he would know that I was "technically" taking his girlfriend home. How would he react, seeing us walk out together? If I looked at him, he would see it in my face. If I looked away, he would know for sure. How to play this?

"I'll meet you at the car. I have to talk to someone," I said as I receded towards the back of the room.

"Who?"

The band exploded into another loud one.

"Billie."

She couldn't hear me. I watched as Monica followed her out. At the door Santo turned away from the tall girl and put his hand out to stop Monica. Nini took Monica by the hand and looked at Santo. Santo backed down and they left. Tough, I thought. Nini could be tough without being anything but herself. Just a look, and he knew she was right.

I looked around for Billie, I really did want to say something to him. I didn't know what, but I wanted to somehow convey what it had meant to me that he had hung out with me all day. I finally found him making out with a girl and decided not to bug him. I stood around for a couple of minutes and then swiftly exited, only briefly glancing at Santo, who didn't even know I existed. He was now kissing the tall girl. Everybody seemed to be scoring tonight …

As I stepped out into the cool night air, I looked back into the chaos. The crowd parted for just a moment and I saw Logan, his dazzling eyes sparkling this way and that as he searched the room for someone … some girl … Nini.

We pulled up to Blake's mom's ranch house in a little cul-de-sac on the East Side. I was in the back, Monica rode shotgun. Nini got out and ran over to the mailbox. She put the envelope inside with a little giggle and turned to run back but a car had pulled in behind us, and its lights were blinding her. She stopped and waited as the car pulled past her and parked in the driveway. It was Blake.

"Hey. What's up?" Blake asked, completely understated, as if he'd been expecting her.

"Hi. I just left a little present for you in the mailbox."

"You guys want to come in? My mom's not home."

No. I didn't.

"OK," Nini said, throwing a smile back at me.

Blake checked the mailbox and pulled out the envelope. He looked at it, then up at Nini. She followed him to the door.

Monica and I sat in the living room, watching MTV and eating American cheese which Blake had hastily tossed to us as Nini waited in his bedroom. He then disappeared down the hall, and we heard the door click shut.

"You like MTV?"

She shrugged.

Motley Crue strutted their stuff.

"MTV doesn't play the kind of music I like," she said quietly.

"What are you into?"

"Velvet Underground. Echo and the Bunnymen. Sex Pistols."

"Oh cool," I replied, happy that I had at least heard the Sex Pistols. "Anarchy in the U.K.," I said, then looked down, feeling dumb. She just sat there, watching Motley Crue.

"What happened with Santo?"

She looked at me straight daggers.

"Sorry."

She thought for a moment, then leaned over and kissed me. Totally surprised, I jumped back.

"Fine," she said and went back to watching TV.

"Sorry, I just … you surprised me. I totally want to kiss you."

After a moment she looked back at me again. We studied each other's faces. Hers was a soft olive, her nose rather large but straight and attractive. Her naturally red lips formed a tight smile. Her wavy, dyed-black hair hung low over her large, but constantly squinted, eyes.

"Your sister told me you're a virgin," she said after a moment.

I was silent. My heart sank. She saw it sink and gently reached over and put her hand on my leg. Gathering strength, I leaned in and we kissed. She was a good kisser. Thankfully, I had now kissed enough to not totally suck, and it was going pretty well. She pulled me back onto her and started unbuckling my belt.

"Fuck, this is it." I thought. "I'm not messing it up this time." I unbuttoned her blouse to reveal small but lovely breasts with erect nipples. She pulled my pants down and I went to work on her labyrinthine belt, which had more straps and buckles than I could undo in the short time we surely had. She did it for me, and I pulled her pants down. Wow. Here we were. I was shaking. I couldn't tell if she could feel it or not, but she didn't say anything. Not like Vishna. I was hard, and she was pulling me toward her. We were going to do this. "What do I do?" I fumbled with her vagina, and she gently stroked me.

Not too much, I thought. I don't want to blow this before it starts. I pushed her hand away from my dick before she made me come. I immediately regretted it. She bit my ear and whispered into it.

"Do you have a condom?"

Fuck.

"No. Do you?"

She shook her head and went slightly limp.

"You're not on the pill?"

"Yeah, I am. But that's not what I'm worried about."

"What are you worried about?"

"AIDS."

"AIDS? I'm not gay …"

She rolled her eyes at me. She was so good at doing that.

"You don't have to be gay."

I took a deep breath and rested my head on her neck, kissing her shoulder. I knew about AIDS. But I didn't know anyone who had it. Not straight people, anyway. One of my mom's gay friends had it. But how would I have gotten it? I was a virgin. How would I have AIDS?

I rubbed my dick on her leg and gently tried to push in. She pushed me back.

"We're not having sex without a condom."

"I'm a virgin. How could I possibly have AIDS?"

"I'm not a virgin. What if Santo gave me AIDS?"

"Santo has AIDS?" My mind quickly flashed to Nini sitting on his bed …

"I don't know. I doubt it. But the point is I only have safe sex. So no condom, no sex."

I thought for a moment.

"Hold on."

I got up and pulled my pants up over my boner. I hopped down the hallway to Blake's door. Music was playing quietly inside — some folky shit. I gently knocked, but there was no response. Desperate, I carefully turned the handle and opened the door a crack. I peered in. Nini was on the bed, her tits flopped into her armpits. There was a blanket over her from her navel down, and I could make out Blake's form down there, his head between her legs. Nini's eyes were rolled back in her head. After a moment of me watching she spotted my eye in the crack of the door.

"What the fuck?" she mouthed.

"I need a condom," I mouthed back, while miming the motion of putting a condom on. Blake began to stir, but she held his head down and he went back to work. She pointed to her little denim purse, which was sitting on a desk by the door. I reached in as she pointed to my boner and mock-laughed. I rifled the purse until I felt the crisp foil wrapper. I held it up. She smiled, and I pulled my arm back and quietly shut the door as Nini's eyes rolled back into her head.

I hopped back down the hallway. I was expecting Monica to have tired of this and put her clothes back on, but to my surprise she had not. She lay there mostly naked, save for her blouse which was open. She looked up at me. I held the condom up and smiled. I sat down next to her and opened it. While I had never used a condom before, I had once put one on for practice — at Nini's suggestion. I pulled the condom out of the package. I rolled it over the head of my dick. I pushed hard a couple of times before realizing something wasn't right. It wouldn't roll down any more. I pulled it off and looked it over. I flipped it over and started again. This time it rolled right on. OK. This is it. I'm ready. I leaned over and kissed her, then tried to get it in. With no luck. She put her hand down there and got me started. I pushed a few times and boom! I was in.

"Marvelous," I blurted.

"What?"

"It feels good," I said, covering.

She pulled her legs around me and put her hand on the back of my head, pulling me in close.

"Deeper."

I tried not to take this as an insult, and pushed in as deep as I could. That felt good. I pushed. I pulled. I pushed. I pulled. I started to ram her as fast as I could. Bam bam bam. I figured I'd try to get her to come, too, before the inevitable.

"Jesus, how long does it take to make a girl come?" I wondered to myself.

I came. Oh. That felt great. I took a deep breath, and as I exhaled, the feeling came. The sister feeling. Fuck. I felt horrid. Her breath, her smell, it all suddenly disgusted me. But she was awesome. What the fuck was wrong with me? She was beautiful, she was my age, she was cool and she liked me. Or at least liked me enough to fuck me. She immediately could tell something was up.

"What?"

I was silent, my face away from hers.

"What's the matter?"

"Nothing. That was awesome." Indeed it was awesome. While it lasted. But now it was agony. I sat up.

"Were you close?"

"Close to what?"

"You know… coming."

She let out a short laugh.

"Yeah, super close."

I couldn't tell if I should believe her or not. But I figured since she laughed, I shouldn't.

"Well, thanks. I'm not a virgin anymore," I said as I turned to her.

She rolled her eyes. She really could convey exactly what she meant by doing that. She meant get off. I did.

She started to put her clothes on. I followed her lead, thankfully.

"Usually it takes guys a few more minutes to want to run away."

Shame. I sat down next to her.

"Have you slept with a lot of guys?"

"Fuck you."

"Sorry."

She was dressed. She leaned back and watched MTV.

"I'm sorry, I really like you … I just. I feel weird. I don't know how to explain it."

"Don't bother. It's no big deal," she said without looking at me.

Twenty or so minutes later Blake and Nini came out of

his room looking sweaty but refreshed, and we split.

I sat in the back on the drive home. Monica and Nini spoke briefly about Santo and that he was such a slut and that Monica should have known it would end this way. Evidently he had screwed the tall girl in the bathroom, and Monica had walked in on them. Santo had called out for her to stay and talk, but had not stopped fucking the girl while he did so. After that I guess he just figured what was done was done.

Nini glanced at me in the rearview often as she and Monica spoke. She comforted Monica, even as I could see her squirming around the fact that she, too, had slept with Santo. Why had she put herself in this position? She could have easily left Monica there, crying at the show. They weren't good friends. Perhaps she was feeling guilty and was trying to make it up to Monica, clandestinely? Perhaps, but I thought of another possible answer, one that was a bit more appealing to me, even though it painted Nini as a bit heartless, which she was not. She had done if for me. She had trapped Monica like a rabbit and tied her up with a bow for me. She had finally helped me lose my virginity. I thanked her with a nod and a smile in the rear view. She gave me an almost imperceptible nod back, and I knew she knew exactly what I meant.

Back at home I watched with regret as Monica followed Nini out to the bus. I felt like an asshole. I had taken advantage of her sadness, given her some crappy virgin sex and then acted like a fool as I wrestled with my weird neurosis. I feared I was really fucked up. Who has sex and then feels like their sexual partner is their sister? I just didn't understand it. I went inside and got in bed. Being alone in my own bed felt good and safe.

About halfway through the Tintin comic I was reading, my door quietly opened. I looked up to find Monica peering in at me. She was in a pair of Nini's pajamas. Red-and-black plaid. She looked sexy in them.

"Nini fell asleep."

"Oh yeah?"

She nodded.

"Can I sleep in here? It's kind of creepy in her bus."

"Sure."

She quickly moved across the room and climbed under the covers.

"So what's the deal?" she asked, squinting judgmentally.

"You mean about earlier?"

"Yeah."

"I don't know. I've had sex like … one-and-a-half times. And both times the same thing happened. I really liked it, then when I was done, I got this super-weird feeling like you were my sister."

"One-and-a-half times? So like, you got a blowjob?"

I nodded.

"And it happened after that, too?"

I nodded again.

"Maybe you're gay."

"I'm not gay."

"How do you know?"

"I just do."

"Does it still feel like I'm your sister now?"

"No. It wears off after about half an hour."

She scooted closer to me, putting her head on my shoulder. She looked at me, our faces very close now.

"Do you want to try again?"

"And what did you say?" Nini asked between sit-ups. She was exercising in the yard just outside of her bus. I sat on the steps of the bus, watching.

"I didn't say anything. We just kissed, and then we did it. Luckily, I still had those condoms you gave me in my drawer."

"Was it good?"

"Yeah, it was great. She got on top and rode me. And I didn't come as fast. Maybe it takes me longer if the girl is on top. Anyway, seems like she knows how to do it better than me, so that worked."

"It's because you already came. Second time always takes longer. As long as it's not too long between times. And so what happened after you came?"

"Same. The second I came I felt super weird. She could tell. She wasn't mad, but maybe disappointed. I slept on the floor."

"Oh my God you're such a dick. If someone did that to me after we had sex I would walk out," she said, but I didn't quite believe her. Being a girl that wasn't ugly, she could pretty much have her pick of sexual partners. Maybe not boyfriends, but she could get most guys to fuck her. But she had outgrown just fucking anyone and now fucked only people she liked. Or thought were interesting. And she wanted these people to like her, too. Or at least find her interesting. She may have been a slut, but she wasn't cavalier about it. She had a love life, not just a sex life. Not that she'd been in love … a love in which she was loved, too … . I knew she had loved Rod, and I was pretty sure she loved Blake. But did they love her? She would do anything for love. Which usually meant sex. Which meant she could be hurt, she could be trampled and she probably wouldn't get up and walk out, even if it meant crying all the way home.

"I know," I replied, ignoring my thoughts about her fragility. "I really like her, too. I mean I really, really like her."

Nini stood up and stretched. I always thought she looked a little funny in her workout clothes — a hooded sweatshirt and shorts. She just didn't look athletic.

"So you just went to bed?"

I nodded as she reached for her toes.

"Yeah. When I woke up she was gone."

"She really wanted to go home bad. Guess you freaked her out. I drove her to her mom's house in Two Rock."

"Two Rock? I thought she lived in Santa Rosa?"

"She just moved in with her mom."

Wow. So she lived out here … . Cool. The weird feeling had passed, and I really liked her again. I thought back to her riding me. It had been great. She had looked down at me with that tight-lipped smile she did when she wanted to smile, but she wasn't feeling generous enough to give you any teeth. Maybe I'd get another chance.

"Maybe you'll get another chance," Nini said, sensing my lust.

"Dude, Blake was totally eating you out when I came in to his room to get a condom." This was our first chance to debrief since the night before, and I wanted the details about the hour or so they spent in his room.

"He loves it. He told me. I could keep him down there all day if I wanted."

"Would you? I mean, is it better than actual sex?"

"It is actual sex."

"You know what I mean." She did.

"No, we had sex after. I don't want to be the only one to come. I'm not a guy."

It took me a moment to figure out what she meant, but I did.

"He told me he loves me."

Oh. I hadn't heard that one before. This was big … or so I guessed.

"Are you serious?" I asked, after some thought.

"Yeah. I told him I love him, too."

"Do you?"

"I think so. Yeah. I do."

JERRY AGAIN, and SIDNEY.

Nini had mostly stopped hanging out downtown in front of the store and was driving into town a couple of times a week to see Blake. I tagged along as often as she'd let me. I'd skate around town or hang around with her and Blake. "Can we stop at the store and grab a soda?" I asked as we pulled out of the driveway and headed down the hill.

"Sure. Get me one, too. Diet Pepsi."

Nini had put on a few pounds, and she was getting self-conscious about her weight to a degree I hadn't seen before.

I got out of the Volvo at the store and went in for the sodas. As I came back out I found Nini chatting with a man who was leaning into her window. As I came around to my side of the car I could see that it was Jerry.

"Hey man. How are ya?" Jerry asked me with a slow smile.

"What's up, Jerry? When did you get back?"

"Just a couple of weeks ago."

He had a mustache — a real mustache bordering on handlebar territory.

"You were gone a long time," I said, staring at the facial

growth.

"Yet," he said, cutting "Yep" so short that the "P" sounded like a "T." "But I'm back."

He smiled at Nini. She was studying his face. Deciding if she still liked it.

"We gotta go," Nini said, starting the car. "But it was really nice to see you."

"Yeah, well, I'm sure we'll bump into each other again soon," Jerry said, his eyes flashing at her. He pulled his head back out of the window and stood up, watching us as Nini backed the car up and we disappeared down the road.

I watched Nini as her gears turned. She did still like his face. I could see the conflict growing inside her already.

"Blake have class today?" I asked, reminding her where we were headed and who she was going to see.

"Yet," she replied, clipping her "P" to a "T" just like Jerry had done.

Poor Blake, I thought, this was not going to go well for him. About halfway into town, Nini fell silent. I knew she was thinking about Jerry. It had taken her aback to see him. I tried to put her mind back on Blake.

"So what does Blake do when he eats you out?"

Nini looked at me like I was insane for a moment, then relaxed.

"Mostly he licks my clit … sometimes he uses his nose."

I thought about this, unable to fathom how he used his nose.

"You know where the clit is, right? I mean … you do, right?"

I was silent for a moment.

"Put your hands like this," she said, making her thumbs and index fingers into a diamond shape resembling a vagina. She showed it to me quickly, then put her hands back on the wheel. I put my hands together and looked at it.

"OK, now where your fingers meet at the top? That's where the clit is, under a little hood."

I stared at the point.

"Under a hood?"

"Yeah, like a little flap of skin."

I couldn't quite picture it.

"I just lick it?"

"Yeah, flick it with your tongue, rub it with your nose … but mostly lick. Not too hard."

"Won't I get hair in my mouth?"

"Probably. Just spit it out, or use your hand."

"And what about pee?"

"She's not going to pee in your mouth."

"But what if there's like, some left over from the last time she peed?" I asked, making a face.

"Dude, do you know how much cum girls drink when guys come in their mouths? You can deal with a tiny bit of pee."

This seemed reasonable to me, though I hoped it wouldn't be the case.

We met Blake in front of the plaza theater and walked up the block to a pizzeria that was on the second floor overlooking the boulevard. We got a window table, and I watched the cars going by below as Nini and Blake exchanged pleasantries and flirted. When the pizza came, Blake and I dug in, but Nini just let her slice sit on her plate, untouched.

"Aren't you gonna eat?" Blake asked.

"I'm not really hungry. I'll nibble at it."

Blake and I finished the rest of the pizza while Nini watched, bored.

"How was class?" Nini asked him, not terribly interested.

"Fine. Junior college is just like high school."

"Same old same old," Nini replied, taking a tiny nibble

of her crust.

"I'm saving up to buy a motorcycle," Blake said out of nowhere.

Nini finally perked up.

"What? A motorcycle? That's crazy. What kind of motorcycle? Like a real, grown-up … motorcycle?"

"Yep."

"How much does a motorcycle cost?" she asked, still trying to digest this surprising news. I watched her as she explored this unlikely notion with her mind. She seemed to be fascinated by the idea.

"I can get something decent, used, for a grand probably. I want a BMW, which are a little more expensive."

"Do you have to have a special license?"

"Yeah, it's a different class. Just gotta take the test."

"How much do you have saved?"

Blake chuckled and looked at me.

"Damn, she's like super interested, huh?"

I shrugged.

"I've probably got enough …"

Nini wasn't listening.

"I bet it's so fun to ride the bay road. Past Marshall …" she said.

She was still thinking of motorcycles, but not Blake's motorcycle. That was clear from her distant look and her eye, which had drifted west.

"You'll be the first person I take for a ride, I promise," he said to her. She smiled.

"Can't wait."

Nini and Blake went back to his house, and I skated the humps for a while by myself. An old maroon Mercedes pulled up at the curb, and the driver lit a cigarette in the darkness of the cab. I kept skating, hoping it wasn't a weirdo or a cop. Finally the driver got out and sat on the hood of his car, watching me and smoking. He was my age, tall and slim, with wingtip shoes and a maroon V-neck sweater that matched his car, over a black t-shirt. His dark hair was slicked back, and he theatrically arched an eyebrow over his large, curved nose whenever I rolled past. After a few passes he pulled a book out of the passenger-side window.

"You want to buy a book?" he said, feigning a deeper voice than he had. I imagined he thought it made him seem cool, or a heavyweight or something. He seemed pretty cool anyway, so I didn't understand why he was putting it on, with the voice and the eyebrow.

"A book? What kind of book?" I asked as I rolled to a stop near him.

"A book I wrote," he said, again raising his eyebrow and holding the book out for me to see. It was a homemade job, spiral bound, maybe 50 pages. On the cover was a photo of him sitting on the hood of his car, arching his eyebrow much like he was doing now. "Ballad of the Philistines and Other Whips and Chains by Sidney Laconico" was written below the photo.

I looked the book over, flipped through the pages. It was poetry. I wasn't into poetry. I thought Nini might like it.

"How much?"

"Fifteen bucks."

"Oh." I pushed the book back towards him.

"Ten Bucks."

"I don't have it."

"Five bucks."

"I have three."

"Jesus Christ kid, that'll barely keep me in smokes and coffee for the night."

"It's all I've got. How old are you?"

"How old do you think I am?"

"Sixteen."

"How old are you?"

"Fifteen. I'll be 16 in a month," I said, resolutely.

"Fine, we'll both be 16 in a month."

"So you're 15? And you drive?"

"No. I'm 16, and in a month we both will be."

I chuckled, which he didn't like.

"Hey, if you don't want the book, don't waste my time."

"No, I want the book."

This made him feel good. He softened.

"Where do you live? I've never seen you around before."

"Tomales."

"Like Tomales out in the boonies? What the hell are you doing here?"

"My sister drove me in. Nowhere to skate out there."

He looked me over.

"Give me the three bucks."

I handed him the money, and he gave me the book.

"Come on, I'll buy you a cup of coffee."

We tooled around town for a little while in his Mercedes, listening to the classical music station. He really took himself seriously, but I liked him. I'd never met someone who wrote a book before, especially someone my age. He put it on really thick, but he was actually cool, which seemed like a paradox. Most people I knew were either cool or they weren't. The ones that tried to be cool weren't, and the cool ones needn't try. He was both cool and trying to be cool at the same time, which made him interesting.

We pulled up in front of the café by the plaza, which was only a block from where we began, and grabbed a table outside. The place was deserted. I waited at the table while he went in and ordered, returning with two cups of black coffee. I didn't drink coffee, but I choked a sip down with a cigarette.

"How you getting home?"

"My sister's gonna pick me up here at nine."

"So what's your sister like?"

"She writes poetry."

He lit up.

"Oh yeah?" But then he faded a little, on the defensive. "Published?"

"Nah."

He perked up again.

"What kind of music does she like?"

"Mostly hippie music."

"Bowie?"

"Yeah, she loves Bowie."

"Cool."

When Nini pulled up to the curb I walked over to the car and leaned in the window.

"Hey, want to park for a few minutes? I want you to meet my new friend."

Nini looked over at Sidney. He arched his eyebrow and nodded to her. I pushed his book in at her.

"He wrote this book. Here, I bought it for you."

She looked the book over. She checked the photo against Sidney's face.

"OK."

Nini parked and walked over.

"You wrote this?"

"That's me on the cover isn't it?"

She sat down. I offered her my coffee, which she took.

"I hear you're a poet, too," Sidney said to her.

"I write poems."

"You like the Beats?"

"You mean Jack Kerouac and those guys?"

"Yeah. Ginsberg, Ferlinghetti."

Nini thought for a second.

"I guess so. But I do my own thing."

"What do you write about?" he asked, leaning in with his cigarette as if he were a reporter, the cigarette perched between his fingers like a microphone.

She thought again. She looked him over. Then she took the cigarette out of his hand and took a drag off of it.

"Love. What else is there?"

He leaned back, impressed. He nodded, as if to say, "You're cool."

He spotted Van the Man locking up the plaza doors.

"You guys gotta get back to the boonies right away or you want to go in on a bottle of Dago red and read some shit?"

I looked at Nini, not knowing what the fuck he was talking about.

"Yeah," she said.

Van bought us a bottle of cheap red wine, and we followed Sidney's Mercedes up some winding streets to the top of a hill where we could look out over the town. We opened the Volvo's tailgate and sat in the back, drinking wine and looking out.

Sidney read first. He read the first chapter of his book, which was an epic poem about brotherhood and youth and writing poems and drinking wine. When he finished he took a long hard swig off the bottle, as if he was exhausted and dehydrated from his long, 10-minute read. He passed it to me and I took a good hit as Nini looked through her notebook for something to read. She read one of her longer poems, one about Bodi that had some graphic sex in it. This seemed to delight Sidney, and he howled at the moon theatrically.

"Yeah!" he shouted. "Dig it!"

I was a little embarrassed by his Beatnik schtick, but also impressed that he was so wholly formed. He had created a persona, and he was living through it. He knew who he was or at least who he was pretending to be, and he was committing to it. In contrast, I hardly knew who I was or even aspired to be. We were the same age. I could tell Nini thought he was cool, too. As she read she periodically looked up to see his reaction. When he hooted or shouted she couldn't help but smile, though she tried to retain her serious, poet-like stature.

When she finished he congratulated her, told her all the lines that he loved about the poem, even embellishing the sex lines. She ate it up. But I was getting tired. It was late, and the red wine was getting to me. I made up an excuse to climb into the front seat, fiddled with the radio for a moment, then, finding the classical station, I looked back to Sidney, who nodded his approval. I turned it up and rested my head against the door.

I woke up to the sound of crying. I looked back through sleepy eyes to see Sidney crying in Nini's arms. I closed my eyes and listened. I must have fallen asleep again, because when I next opened my eyes Nini and Sidney were laughing hysterically at something. I closed my eyes again.

When I awoke again I fully expected them to be getting it on in the back of the Volvo but instead found them sitting in the same place discussing e.e. cummings, who it turned out was mutually their favorite poet. I looked at the clock — I had slept for an hour.

"Hey man, your sister is cool. You know that, right?"

"She's alright," I said with a smile as I climbed out of the car and took a piss facing the lights of the town.

"You like him?" I asked, rolling the window down and putting my arm out as we hit a fog bank just outside of Tomales. I loved the feeling of the damp fog on my hand.

"I love him. We professed our love to each other."

"Are you serious?"

"Yes. We're kindrid spirits. We have 'kismet.' We're

platonic lovers."

"Platonic?" I asked, not at all sure what this meant, but it sounded kind of kinky. "What did you guys do?"

"Nothing. Platonic means without sex. We're lovers, but we don't have sex. We commune through our poetry."

"Why?" I asked.

Nini thought for a moment.

"I guess he didn't want to fuck me."

I looked at her for a moment. OK. I got it. And anyway, they had communed. I felt like Sidney and I had in some way as well. Maybe not on such a high plane, but we liked each other. He had bowed to me when we parted ways. I had felt compelled to bow in return, and I had a feeling we would be friends if not platonic lovers …

A few days later Nini and I sat in front of the store, hoping someone would show up. The Volvo had broken down, and we were stuck. Nini hadn't been to see Blake since the night we met Sidney, and I guess he was getting nervous because he called a lot.

After a half hour or so Jerry pulled up in his truck. He parked beside us and grinned out at Nini. We were happy to see him, anybody.

"What's up, Nini? Haven't seen you much down here."

"My car broke down, nowhere else to go."

"You need a ride somewhere?"

"No, we're just hanging out. What are you doing?"

"Same."

He got out and went into the store.

"Do you think he noticed?"

"What?"

"That I've gained weight."

"You're crazy."

She had gained a couple of more pounds, but even I wouldn't have noticed if she hadn't pointed it out to me several times a day. She had been fretting that Blake would be disgusted with her the next time they met, especially because it had been a few days.

Jerry came out with three RC colas, handed us each one. Then he leaned up against his truck and took a long swig, all the while keeping his eyes on Nini.

"Thanks," we said, in unison.

"Jinx, you owe me a coke!" I shouted. Nini ignored me.

I could tell Nini was uneasy. She was drawn to Jerry. He had an earthy manliness that couldn't be denied. He moved slowly and spoke only what was necessary. A bold contrast to all the high-strung kids we had been hanging out with; even Sidney, who was by far the most adult-seeming 16-year-old I had encountered.

"I feel like we have some unfinished business," Jerry finally said, surprising both Nini and me.

"Yeah? Like what?" she said, betraying no sense of interest or disinterest. Just totally matter of fact. It left him flapping in the wind. I think he had expected her to swoon. Which was unexpected, since he was usually so unassuming.

He changed tacks.

"I really missed you while I was gone."

She looked him over. Her eye drifted. Her guard fell like a curtain.

"I missed you, too. How come you stayed away so long?"

"Opportunity. When it knocks, you gotta open the door." He took a long sip from his soda, hoping his meaning would come across in the silence. It did.

"I have a boyfriend now," she said, lamenting.

He didn't react. After a moment he took another long swig off of his soda, finishing it. He tossed the empty bottle in the back of his truck.

"Friend of mine?"

"No. He's from Petaluma."

Jerry thought again.

"Let's go for a drive."

"Where to?"

He was caught off guard once again. He had expected a yes-or-no answer to a yes-or-no question. Finally he dove in.

"My house."

Nini contemplated this.

"We can't have sex."

He smiled and looked away, a little embarrassed that the conversation had finally come completely out into the open, especially with me present.

"I never made you my seafood lasagna," he said, attempting to circle back to his "unfinished business" line with a closed grin. It worked.

Nini went off with him to make lasagna, and I sat on the curb contemplating my next move. I remembered that Monica was living in Two Rock.

I walked up to the house and grabbed my old bike and set out to find her, pedaling through the rolling green hills past broken-down barns and wood fences, rows of tall eucalyptus and fields of grazing sheep.

Half an hour later I reached the crossroads that stood in for a town known as Two Rock. In each direction a couple of old farmhouses lingered. I headed west first, coming to an old gray house with some chicken coops beside it. I stopped and looked over the place. Suddenly an enormous German shepherd came running at me full bore. I tried to find the pedal, but stumbled. I looked back up just as it leapt into the air, headed straight for my face, its face a mess of teeth, slobber and fiery eyes. YANK. It snapped back and fell to the ground, its chain reaching its limit. I stood there for a moment trying to catch my breath, shaking uncontrollably as the dog growled and slobbered.

I pedaled on.

The next house I came to was a newer place, maybe built in the '60s. Ranch style. I looked around for dogs, then rode up to the front door, got off and knocked. No answer. I knocked again, louder this time. Finally an old man in overalls and no shirt or shoes opened the door. He had longish gray hair and a tattoo of a ship on his forearm.

"Hi, is Monica here?" I asked, deciding to forgo the explanations.

"Monica? No Monica here."

He looked me over, then nodded as if he had figured me out.

"But I did notice a little chick around your age moved in with Tom and his girlfriend down the street. Sexy thing."

Surprised by his forthrightness, I looked past him into the house for clues as to what kind of dude I was talking to. I could only make out a couple of modern paintings and a bottle of gin on a side table. The bottle was open, and a half-full glass was beside it.

"Black hair? Kind of punk?" I asked, betting he'd know what I meant.

"I don't know punk, but she seems a little rock and roll if that's what you mean." He smiled, revealing a silver front tooth. "I know rock and roll."

"Which house was it?" I asked, growing nervous that this would get weird eventually. Old hippie dirt-farmer dudes out here were usually starved for companionship, and I didn't want to get stuck playing chess and drinking gin with this old fucker, all the while wondering if he'd turn his libidinous attentions to me. I had encountered more than one old man like him who eventually decided a young man like me was better than nothing and made a move. I was good at escaping unscathed and usually knew them well enough to remind the drunk bastards what they had to lose by crossing the line, but I didn't know this guy at all.

"You into rock and roll?" he asked. "I play the sax. You ever heard of The Stone? It's a club in the city. I played there last night with Jerry Garcia." He waited for my response.

Here we go, I thought.

"Yeah, but I'm really trying to find this girl."

"That's cool, man. I'm just bored. My old lady is in Idaho with her sister, and I've just been sitting here drinking gin all day by myself. When you knocked I thought you were my weed man. But when I saw you I thought, hey maybe this kid is cool."

I could see he was lonely, but I just wasn't into it today. I liked old dudes that liked to talk. I liked to listen to their stories, learn about the good old days. But today I was on a mission.

"That's cool, man. Thanks. I really just gotta find this girl."

"That's cool, that's cool. I saw her over at Tom's place. Just past Twin Bridges Road there. Red house." He pointed back the way I had come.

"Thanks." I pedaled off.

"You guys get bored you can come by. I've got some weed coming ..." he yelled after me.

I rode up to the two-story red farmhouse. Its paint was faded, and it looked a little crooked — like it was leaning into the earth. I leaned my bike up against a tree and walked to the door and knocked. After a moment I heard footsteps, and the door opened. Monica peered out at me. Her lips tightened into a coy smile, and her eyes narrowed.

"Hey. What are you doing here?" she asked.

"I came to find you," I said, trying to judge just how much heroic spin I should include.

"Well, looks like you found me," she said. She waited, still smiling, for my reply.

"What are you up to?" I asked. Boring.

"Eating lunch. You hungry?"

Nice. More than I had expected.

"Sure."

She showed me into the house. It looked like many of the farmhouses in the area — it hadn't been updated since the '50s or '60s. No new technology except for a TV stacked haphazardly on an old dresser. Tidy but not clean. Monica was very out of place here. This was Old World, sedentary. Everything about Monica was not. Not to me, anyway. She was town, she was rock and roll like the man had said. But here she was. She made me a cheese sandwich, and we sat on the couch.

"How'd you find me?"

"I just rode out and knocked on a couple doors. Weird guy across the road said he'd seen a girl my age move in with 'Tom.'"

"Tom's my stepdad," she said, which I interpreted to be a defensive move assuring me it was not a boyfriend. I was encouraged.

"That's what I figured," I said, putting that to bed. "How do you like it here?"

She smiled that tight lipped, pursed smile.

"It sucks. What do you think?"

I laughed.

"What do you do out here all day."

"You're looking at it."

We were silent for a moment.

"I'm really sorry about … last time …"

"What about the time before that?" she asked, deadpan.

"Yeah, sorry for that, too. I don't know what's wrong with me, I really don't. But I feel like it's not permanent. I think it's gonna go away."

"You better hope it does," she replied, her teeth breaking

through her lips in a wide smile. She pulled out a pack of cigarettes from her pocket. "Come on, let's have a smoke."

I finished the last bite of my sandwich and followed her out.

Outside we sat on a couple of old wicker chairs and looked out over the fields while we smoked.

"Where's Nini?"

"She's down in Marshall, making lasagna."

"Is that like, code or something?" she asked, nudging me with her toe.

"In this case, no. Or I don't think so, anyway."

"Your sister really likes sex, huh?"

"I guess so. Who doesn't?"

"You?"

She had me there. I did like sex, but the aftermath was really messing me up.

"I do like it … . Maybe I just don't like … after," I said, then looked away.

"Maybe if you didn't finish … ?"

I was horribly embarrassed, but also it was somehow comforting to talk about it with someone who seemed so nonchalant, even after being the victim of it.

"That would probably be really frustrating."

"Yeah, probably."

We were silent for a moment. I leaned back in my chair and felt the warmth of the sun's rays penetrating my body. I felt good. I felt like we were getting to know each other.

"What about you?" I asked, feeling very comfortable and self-assured.

"What?

"Do you like sex?"

"I think you already know the answer to that."

I guess I did.

"Where are your parents?"

"They went to Tom's parent's house."

"Do you want a massage?"

She looked at me for a long time. Perhaps a full minute. She studied my face, then my hands. She looked at my crotch. The sun beat down on my face, and I felt a bead of sweat roll down my cheek.

"Are you good at giving massages?" she asked, finally. No smile.

"Really good." I was. I had been giving my mother massages nearly every day for years. Shoulders and feet were my specialty.

"OK."

She took me to her room, which was an odd mixture of punk show flyers and lacy scarves and scented candles. She pulled the curtains closed, which cast a soft red light across the room, and lit one of the candles. She took her shirt off, leaving her bra on, then laid down on her stomach. She reached around and unclasped her bra, then closed her eyes.

"OK."

I sat on her butt and began to rub her shoulders. She had wonderfully soft, tan skin.

"Tell me if I do it too hard."

"I like it hard."

I worked my way down her spine to her lower back, then up the sides, slowly reaching further around until I could feel the very edges of her small breasts, which were squishing out. I rubbed her neck, then worked her shoulders again. I could tell she was enjoying it from her breath, which was long and measured. She turned her head from one side to another and I gathered her hair and moved it for her. She took my hand and pulled it down towards her face. She put my thumb in her mouth and began to suck on it. I got an instant boner and leaned over and began kissing her back. She turned over, and we kissed. I really liked the way she kissed. Very little tongue. When I tried to tongue her, she pushed it back out with her lips. I figured out quickly that she wasn't into that, and followed her lead, sucking on her bottom lip. We eventually got our clothes off, and after a moment of panic as she looked for a condom in her nightstand, we began screwing. She put her hands on my ass and showed me the rhythm she wanted. I followed her lead. There was an unspoken understanding that developed — she was showing me how she wanted it. I was following her. Which was fine with me because I was acutely aware of my inexperience, and ineptitude, as a lover. She kept me going very slowly for some time, then gradually increased my speed. After a few minutes we were moving together, in time. She moved her hands up to the small of my back and continued cueing me, but in a much more subtle way. I sped up. She didn't slow me so I figured it was time. I was really moving now. Our sweaty bellies slapped together and our gyrations synched even closer, our pelvises wriggling back and forth like a washing machine. Boom. I came. I kept pounding away as she let out a wonderful sigh and tightened her grip around my waist. I finally stopped and dropped onto her, out of breath.

"You did it!" she exclaimed.

I had done it. I had fucked. Not just put it in and wiggled, but really fucked.

"Did you come?" I asked.

She smiled.

"No, but I was close. And that's pretty good, for me."

"You don't usually come?"

"Not that way."

I thought about this, realizing after a moment what she probably meant.

"Next time …" I said, hopefully.

She smiled and nuzzled my shoulder with her nose. I took a deep breath and looked up to the ceiling.

I felt fine. I felt fine! I realized that the weird sister-feeling had not come.

"I didn't get it."

"What?" she said, still nuzzling me.

"That weird feeling. I feel great, and I don't want to get out of bed, or away from you. I feel great!"

She smiled.

"Maybe you were just feeling guilty for being a shitty fuck."

I took offense. She saw it in my face, but before she could react, I decided she was right. I probably was a shitty fuck. But not anymore, at least not that shitty. She had taught me how to fuck, and it was a lesson I was sure I would not forget.

The ride home was easy. I pumped up and glided down the hills totally carefree. I thought about having sex with Monica. It really had been awesome. But why hadn't I had the same reaction? Why did I feel so good afterwards? No dread, no creepy sister feelings. Just the joy of feeling totally satisfied. Was it the setting? Her room? No I thought, that didn't matter. Just as I reached Tomales and the sun was setting I came upon a notion that I quickly adopted as the truth. I had gotten to know her. Every time I had gotten the feeling it had come after having sex with a virtual stranger. I kind of knew Monica now. We even had a little bit of a shorthand, knowing where each other was going in conversation. I knew what might bring out her little impish smile, and she seemed to read me like an open book. Maybe we knew each other, and maybe that's what it took for me to enjoy sex. At least for now. I was happy with that explanation and hoped to test it again soon.

As I climbed the hill to our house I noticed a truck

parked out front. Jerry's truck. I pulled my bike in the gate and looked over to Nini's bus. There was only a dim light on, and all the curtains were drawn. Interesting. I put my bike away and went inside.

I ate lasagna with my mother and my little sister, who informed me that Nini and Jerry had returned home with the cooked lasagna and then had gone to the bus where Nini had something she wanted to show Jerry. They had not returned. The lasagna was good, and I went for a second helping. As I scooped it onto my plate, I heard a rumbling. My little sister looked out the window.

"Someone's here," she said, noting the obvious.

Yes, but who? I thought.

The three of us watched through the window as a man wearing a motorcycle helmet entered through the gate and began to walk towards Nini's bus across the darkened yard.

"Who is it?" my sister asked.

"I don't know. A friend of Nini's probably," said my mother.

"Should I go out there?" I asked to no one in particular. No one answered. We watched as the man stepped up to the bus and tried the handle. It didn't open. He knocked. Nothing happened. He knocked again. Finally the door opened, and Nini swung out. She was naked, wrapped in a sheet. Before he noticed, the man in the helmet made a kind of "Ta Da!" motion with his outstretched arms. Then he froze. He took the helmet off, revealing Blake's weary face. We watched as they talked. Nini wouldn't allow him inside. She finally motioned for him to go into the house. We scrambled back to our seats and waited. Blake knocked on the door.

"Come in," my mother said, loudly.

Blake came in. His face was ashen. He tried a weak smile.

"Hey. Nini said to wait in here with you guys. Is that

OK?"

"Of course," my mother said.

"What's wrong?" my sister asked, oblivious to what we had inferred from the window.

"I'm not sure," Blake responded. "I guess I'm gonna find out."

"Are you hungry? There's plenty of lasagna. It's really good. Nini and … her friend made it," Mom said, immediately regretting it.

"No, I'm OK. Thanks."

I was glad he declined and saved himself the embarrassment of eating his rival's creation.

After a few minutes of small talk, my sister ran to the window and reported back.

"Jerry's leaving. He's walking towards the gate now. He opened the gate and is gone."

I looked at Blake. He stayed put. Not even looking to the window for a hint of who Jerry was. I guess he felt better not knowing. A moment later Nini entered. Clothed, but looking freshly fucked. She shut the door behind her, then leaned against it.

"Hi," she said, looking at Blake with a long face. She looked at the helmet he was still holding.

"So you bought a motorcycle?"

He nodded.

"What did you get?" she asked.

"BMW R60," he replied. He seemed satisfied to let the conversation stay off the obvious business at hand.

"Can I see it?" Nini asked.

"Sure."

We all followed Blake out through the gate to the street where his brown BMW was parked. We all acted very impressed. My younger sister asked to sit on it. Blake put her on it for a couple of minutes. Nini said she was really happy for him. Then he put his helmet on. Nini asked him if he wanted to stay and talk, but he declined and rode off into the night.

"I couldn't help myself. I promised myself I wouldn't even kiss him, and I didn't, at his house anyway. We made lasagna and … Jerry is really funny. You probably haven't seen that side of him, because he's so quiet, but he sees the world in a funny way. He makes me laugh. While the food was baking we took his little skiff out and rowed around in the bay. Watched the pelicans. He told me about his trip to Baja. We were having such a nice time. And he never even tried to kiss me. It was like it used to be. Like friends, except there is an electricity between us. It's always there. After we finished baking we put the lasagna in the truck, and he drove me home. He wanted to see my bus. He'd never seen it before. So I showed him. Once we were inside I just pounced on him. I don't know why, I couldn't control myself. I didn't know what he'd do, but he just totally rolled with it, like he'd just been waiting for me to make the first move, which is so not him. I don't get it. Maybe because I'm younger than him? But he was totally into it." She stopped and thought for moment.

I stoked the fire in the potbelly. She went on.

"It was like having sex in slow motion, he's so strong, and moved like everything was planned out. His hands and mouth only went exactly where they should go. It was like a movie. You know in movie sex scene, where they don't mess up, or fumble, they just do it perfectly? Totally passionate. And he lasted like an hour. I came. I came so hard. It was rad."

"So what about Blake?"

She took a deep breath.

"I love Blake."

"That's what I thought."

She started to cry. It had finally caught up with her. Now that the sex and the telling of the sex was over, she knew she had fucked up.

"Do you think he was mad? Or just sad?" she asked in vain, through the tears.

"I don't know."

"You know, I knew Jerry first. I was with him first. We just never fucking had sex, which was driving me crazy."

I was silent, knowing that this did not matter.

"Blake is so sweet. I can't believe he showed up. I mean what the fuck? He could have called first."

"I guess he wanted to surprise you with the bike …?" I replied, apologetically.

"Yeah. He's so sweet. I can't believe I did this to him. I'm such a bitch. I told him, you know, that I wouldn't. He knows every guy I've slept with. I told him. And he told me. He's only slept with two other girls, but still. And he said he wouldn't fuck anyone else, too. I never thought in a million years he'd just show up. I thought I'd just be able to forget it, compartmentalize it. I'm such a bitch. I probably broke his heart. He's so sweet, this probably broke his fucking heart." She sobbed more.

I lit a cigarette and watched her cry for a little while, then she looked at me and reached out for it. I handed it to her, and she took a long drag. She began to think. I watched her eyes search the room for clues. What to do? Was there a way out of this? After a couple of minutes she seemed to have a thought. She handed me back the cigarette and climbed down from her high bed.

"I guess it wasn't true love, because if it was I wouldn't have wanted to fuck Jerry. Right?"

I shrugged. I didn't know.

A couple of days later I was sitting on the front porch, waiting for Nini to get home from school. She was attending junior college in Santa Rosa. Some days she would come back and we'd do something, somedays she would stay out late with Franny, who was giving her a ride since the Volvo was out of commission.

I heard the sound of a motorcycle pull up outside the gate, beyond the hedge. Blake, I thought. Bad timing again. She's not here, dude. Why don't you ever call?

The gate opened and Nini stood there, helmet in hand. Oh. This is a development. I waited for Blake to follow her in. She beckoned me towards her. Curious, I walked out the gate, past her and looked. A BMW motorcycle. But not Blake's. This one was black. There was no one else there. What the fuck? I turned back to Nini.

"What the fuck? Did you ride that motorcycle here?"
She smiled.
"Whose is it?" I asked, incredulous.
"Mine. I just bought it."
"Are you serious? You bought a motorcycle?"
She nodded.
"Want to go for a ride?" she asked.
"Do I get to ride in front?"
"No. You don't know how to ride a motorcycle."
"And you do?"
"I do now. Just took my test."
She climbed on the bike. She really had to climb. It was much too tall for her. She could only touch with one foot at a time, and just the tippy-toe of that foot, with her ass on the seat. She almost dropped the bike but caught it with my help, and together we righted it.
"Get on."
I climbed on the back, and she started the bike. She put it in gear. We teetered a little, then she hit the gas, released the clutch and we bolted out onto Hwy 1. She wasn't bad. I was in total awe. How had my sister learned how to ride

a motorcycle so quickly? I held on tight as she swung the bike into the first curve of the bay road. We cruised for a few miles, then she turned around and we road back home.

In front of the gate I climbed off, but she kept her helmet on.

"That was awesome! I can't believe you bought that!?"

"I'm going to Blake's," she said, through the partially opened visor.

"Oh!" I said, surprised. As far as I knew she hadn't spoken to him since he had ridden off on his bike.

"Does he know you're coming?"

She shook her head.

"I'm gonna surprise him with the bike. If he's got a girl in bed with him when I show up, then we're even. If he doesn't, then we can talk and maybe go for a ride. Good plan, right? I mean, who could resist a girl on a motorcycle?"

I nodded and watched her ride off, hopelessly jealous of her new wheels.

I called Monica. After some badgering she agreed to get her mom to drive her over. I introduced her to my mom and younger sister. They all seemed to get along great, and my mom invited her to eat dinner with us. After dinner I took her to my room. She had had the foresight to tell her mom she was staying over with Nini. We talked for a while, and then she suggested we go to bed.

We kissed for a long time. I felt no pressure to rush into it. We both knew what was coming, and that had a calming effect on me.

"Have you ever eaten a girl out?" she asked as I nuzzled her neck. This was not what I was expecting.

"No."

"Want to give it a try?"

"Sure."

I kissed her neck, then moved down over her breasts to

her waist. She still had her pants on, which I unbuckled, then pulled down. I put my face between her legs. She smelled like strawberries, the residue of her shampoo, I figured. I appreciated the effort. I tried to think back to the lesson Nini had given me. I pushed my tongue out and licked the closed labia of her vagina. The slight taste of urine gave me pause, but I decided I could work through it, and it dissipated after a moment. I hunted around for the clitoris, remembering that it should be at the top. After fumbling around, licking her labia with no effect, I moved up and my tongue slid over a pebble-sized bump. This must be it, I thought. I began to lick it, and Monica immediately responded by arching her back and letting out a big sigh. I went to town, licking away until she pulled me up and put me inside her. I was thankful, as my tongue was tired. It felt as though the little tab of skin that holds the tongue to the bottom of the mouth was about to tear from overextension. Alright, lesson learned, I guess. We gyrated together. Afterwards, as we lay there catching our breath, she turned to me and smiled with her tight-lipped, impish smile.

"Not bad for your first try," she said.

"Yeah? Nini kind of explained to me how to do it."

"She's a good teacher. A lot of guys think the point is to fuck you with their tongue."

I wondered how many guys had done it to her.

Late that night after we had both fallen asleep, I awoke to the sound of two bikes pulling up and stopping. So it worked, I thought to myself. I peeped out the window and watched Blake and Nini walk in through the gate, helmets in hand, and go into her bus. Very good, I thought.

I turned back to Monica and was caught off guard by the image of her naked body. The blankets had come off and she lay very still on her back, her entire body exposed. It was a full moon and the soft pale light landed brilliantly on her lovely young form, turning her a mesmerizing silver color. Her nipples were erect from the cold, and her face was relaxed, almost smiling. Her belly button created a dark pool in the moonscape between the gentle slopes of her pelvis. A small strip of pubic hair curved down between her slender-but-firm thighs, perfectly punctuating her cello-like curves. I sat staring at her for a long while, hoping the image would be burned into my memory forever. I knew this was worth savoring. Finally, I slid in next to her warm body, pulled the covers up and closed my eyes. All was well … for the night, anyway.

JACK.

I went out to Nini's bus and knocked. It was early afternoon, and we hadn't seen her in the house. I knocked a couple of times, but there was no answer. I opened the door and peeked in. Nini was lying in bed, her eyes open, staring at the wall.

"Hey. You OK?"

She didn't respond.

"Nini?"

Finally she turned her eyes to me, without moving her head. We looked at each other for a moment or two.

"What's wrong?"

She took another moment.

"Nothing. Just don't feel like getting up."

"Are you bummed out?"

She shrugged.

"Have you eaten breakfast?"

She didn't answer.

I had seen her like this before. Many times. Down a deep hole. I was ill equipped to help her climb out, but sometimes tried to at least distract her.

"Is it Blake?"

She shook her head.

"Someone else?"

"Can you leave me alone?" she said and turned away from me, burying her face in the pillow.

I sighed.

"You should get up."

"Fuck you."

I turned and shut the door. I looked around the yard. My new-to-me Triumph motorcycle sat beside her BMW in the driveway. I walked over, put the kickstand up, then pushed it over to the door of the bus. I kicked it over and revved it up. It was loud. I had pulled the mufflers off of it and put straight pipes on. I revved some more and waited.

After a few minutes of idling and intermittent revving, Nini came to the door. She was dressed now, all in black. She had her helmet under her arm. I said nothing, just dropped it into first and motored over to her bike. Nini followed. She climbed on her bike beside me in the driveway and put on her helmet.

"You want to take Marshall-Petaluma Road? It's more fun than Bodega Highway," I said, then revved it again for effect.

Usually it was very difficult to pull Nini out of a hole once she had entered one, and she could stay there for days. But the thought of leaning through some tight corners, gunning it down the coast and not crashing was just so exciting that she couldn't resist.

"OK," she responded, and popped her clutch, bolting out in front of me. We both sped up the driveway and onto Hwy 1, heading south. I pulled up next to her as we rolled through downtown. A couple of kids waved to us with limp, envious waves. I couldn't help but smile. I had finally gotten my own bike, and riding beside Nini filled me with pride. We were cool, I thought. How could we not be? Two teenage kids roaring through town on all that chrome and aluminum …

We hit the bay road and began leaning through its snake-like turns. I let Nini set the pace. She kept it swift, but safe. After a couple of miles I got cocky and passed her on the inside of a turn that she took a little slow, upping the pace, leaning hard into the curves. She kept up. At Marshall-Petaluma Road we turned left, and I slowed to let her come up beside me.

"Did you see me scrape my peg in that hairpin by the oyster farm?" I asked, showing off.

She nodded, then pointed to the left-side cylinder-head cover of her bike's motor. It had horizontal scrapes across much of it.

"You scraped?"

She smiled and nodded again. Scraping one's cylinders on a BMW was a sign of hard, fast riding. A badge of courage.

I smiled back and gunned it.

About half way into town a disheveled kid with no helmet or glasses pulled up beside us on a straightaway. Nini wore a full-face helmet, her long, blonde ponytail hanging out the back, but I just wore sunglasses to keep the bugs and wind out of my eyes. This guy had tears running out of his eyes, back into his hair. He nodded as he pulled up between us, gently forcing his way in.

"Nice bikes!" he yelled above the roar. He was riding a Kawasaki rat bike, spraypainted flat black. It paled in comparison to our shiny, vintage European bikes. Instead of a leather jacket he wore an old t-shirt over which a ragged flannel shirt flapped in the wind behind him. His dirty jeans had holes in the knees. He wore no gloves and instead of the heavy leather boots, he wore Chuck Taylors. He looked about 18.

We both nodded to him, keeping our cool, but giving

each other a quick, annoyed look.

"Cool if I ride with you guys?" he yelled.

I shrugged. Nini nodded.

"I'm Jack!"

We rode the rest of the way into town as a threesome, each jockeying for first position, then ceding the position to another and so on until we reached Petaluma, pulling up at Blacky's Café.

Blake and a tall, lanky kid with blond hair named Bart were sitting at an outside table, drinking coffee and smoking. Bart's Triumph 500 was parked beside Blake's BMW.

We parked our bikes. Nini pulled her helmet off, and I watched as Jack caught his first glimpse of her face. She was striking in all black, her blonde hair contrasted against it. He took a deep breath. I could tell he was already into her. How could he not be? A cute little chick riding a big BMW, keeping up with the boys through the curves. I liked Jack's face. It was round and soft, with tiny shallow wrinkles in his forehead and around his mouth. His chin was weak, but he had friendly blue eyes that sparkled in the sunlight.

"You want some coffee?" Jack asked her, ignoring the rest of us.

"OK," Nini replied, showing no hint of the dark cloud she had been under at home.

He smiled, and as he walked away his bike slowly leaned, then fell over, crashing on the sidewalk. He had forgotten to put his kickstand down. He looked at the bike for a moment, then decided it was cooler to leave it. He shrugged and walked in to order. We all laughed. Watching Nini laugh gave me a great sense of comfort. The ride had worked. Today would be OK.

"Who's that dude?" Blake asked, a little defensive.

"No clue, we ran into him near Marshall and he asked if

he could ride with us," I said as I pulled out a cigarette and offered one to Bart, who accepted, flicking his Zippo open and lighting us both. Bart was Blake's neighbor. He and I had become fast friends when we both decided to give up skateboarding for motorcycling, forming something of a teenage bike gang with Nini, Blake and a couple of other guys who hung out at the café. He was into rockabilly music and had a rare disease that made one side of his jaw grow longer than the other. It gave his face a curve that had a half-moon-like quality.

"His bike's leaking gas," Bart said, blowing out a drag of smoke.

Indeed, the overturned bike was leaking from its carburetor. Blake got up and picked the bike up, resting it on its kickstand.

Jack came out and sat down beside Nini in Blake's seat. He handed her a coffee.

"Oh thanks, man," Jack said to Blake, who grabbed another chair and scooted in near Nini.

"You were leaking gas."

"Oh shit. I'm surprised I had any left," he said, then turned to Nini. "So cool I ran into you guys. I never ride out there, but I had a wedding to go to in Stinson Beach. These roads are killer. Reminds me of Santa Cruz. Switchbacks forever. I thought I was lost when I found you guys, and I was sure I'd run out of gas."

I looked over his ragged clothes, then looked at Nini, who was thinking the same thing.

"You wore that to a wedding?" she asked, smiling. Her eye was drifting, and I could see he was trying to figure out which one to look into. His lips curled up in the hint of a smile, and I saw that he found it charming.

"My mom. She doesn't care. It's her fourth, anyway."

Nini noticed that Blake was looking uncomfortable and

handed him her coffee. He took a sip as he eyed Jack, who seemed oblivious to his jealousy.

Blake was still chafing after Nini had ended their year-long romance, citing "freedom' as her reason. They were determined to remain friends, but Blake visibly longed for her whenever they were together, which was still a considerable amount. I was in a similar boat. Monica and I had finally broken up after months of turmoil resulting from my increasingly strong appetite for other girls. Nini had soothed both of us, caring for Monica in her moment of misery when she discovered my infidelity, and did the same for me when I discovered Monica had paid me back in kind.

"Where you from?" I asked.

"I'm from Santa Cruz, but I'm living in Cotati," Jack said. Cotati was a shitty little burg about 10 miles north of Petaluma.

"That sucks," Blake said, trying to be funny but obviously feeling challenged.

"It's alright. Where do you live?" Jack asked, looking at Nini.

"We live in Tomales."

He didn't respond, so she explained, pointing to me.

"He's my brother. We live 15 miles west, almost to the beach."

"Cool. I'll have to come out for a hang."

Nini smiled at his forthrightness as Sidney bounced up. He was wearing a thrift-store suit with an ascot instead of a tie, and an old army bag was slung over his shoulder.

"Nini, you look fucking cool in all black, you know that? Fucking hot biker chick, I dig it. Just like that French movie with what's-her-name on the motorcycle."

"Someone cut your tie off?" Bart asked, sarcastically.

"It's an ascot, man," Sidney replied. He was easily thrown

off his game by sarcasm.

"Oh. It's an assss cot?" Bart said and laughed.

"Fuck you, Bart," Sidney fired off, recovering.

"I'm just messing with you, Mikey," Bart said with a sly grin.

This infuriated Sidney. He and Bart had gone to school together, and Bart still liked to call him by his given name, just to fuck with him.

Sidney reached into his shoulder bag and pulled out a copy of his book.

"See that? That's my name. Sidney Laconico. I haven't been Mikey for three years. Got it?"

Bart laughed.

"I got it. Whatever you say."

"Anybody want to buy a book?" Sidney asked, displaying the book for all to see. He never wasted an opportunity to show it off. There were no takers.

We all shot the shit for a little while, then Sidney suggested we go to his "office." When we all got up to leave, Jack stayed seated. Nini turned back to him before she donned her helmet.

"You want to come?"

He did.

It really was an office, Sidney just didn't use it as one. It was more of a clubhouse. He had made a couple of chapbooks in there with his "publishing partner," a kid named Thelonious who was the grandson of some famous poet, but mostly he just hosted parties and impromptu jam sessions with other kids who could play guitar or tap the bongos.

We passed around a jug of wine, and Sidney played his guitar — backed by Blake on lead. He sang a song he had written about Lenny Bruce. We all knew the song and would chime in for the choruses. The place was sparsely decorated with some flyers from poetry readings, a broken desk and chair, some wine bottles with candles shoved in them and used as candelabras, and an old manual typewriter. The same model Nini used. Sidney and Nini had really bonded over this when Nini and I first came to the office for a "reading" that Sidney was hosting. He was also reading. Eight kids showed up, which, in such a tiny office, didn't seem too bad.

Nini passed the bottle to Jack, who took a big swig. He fit right in, though there was a little tension between him and Blake, which he was just now starting to pick up on. Blake had been staring at him between chord changes.

"What's with him? He keeps staring at me," Jack asked as he passed me the bottle.

"He's just a little jealous. He and Nini used to go out," I said as Sidney ended the song.

"Ahh," Jack said, seemingly unconcerned. He turned back to Nini.

"So you go to school? What do you do?" he asked her.

"I go to the JC and I work at a deli down the street," she replied. "What about you?"

"I'm an apprentice metalworker. I'm learning how to weld."

"Oh. That's cool," Nini said, then turned to Sidney.

"Play the one about the girl who rubs everyone, but rubs them the wrong way," she shouted.

Interesting, I thought. The metalwork stuff had turned her off. She was in a serious artistic period in her life, but she was also becoming aware politically and this kind of union-strong, work-with-your-hands stuff usually got her excited to talk. Sidney began the song, with Blake joining in, and Nini turned back to Jack.

"But what do you 'do'? Welding is work. What do you do?"

"Like art and shit?" he asked.

She nodded.

"Like art and shit."

"Weld."

She just stared at him, her eye drifting badly. Alcohol always made it worse.

"I make shit. Art and shit. Out of metal."

"Oh," she said, then took a long pause, contemplating this. "That's cool."

He pulled a crumpled photo out of his pocket and handed it to her. I craned my neck to see. It was a photo of him standing next to some kind of crude metal sculpture. Nini looked at it for a while before handing it back. She smiled.

"That's really cool. You're a sculptor."

"I don't like to sound pretentious."

"Never miss a chance to sound pretentious!" Sidney shouted between verses of the pretentious song he was singing. Jack smiled and blushed.

"I'd like to see your sculptures some time," Nini said, reaching for the wine and taking a long swig.

"You want to go right now?" Jack asked, then looked around to see who had heard. I had, and it seemed like Bart had, as he was now studying Jack with a renewed interest. Bart was protective of Nini, who he had quickly adopted as a kind of surrogate little sister when he and I began hanging out and riding together. He was over a foot taller than her so "little" seemed accurate.

Nini looked around, too. She looked at Blake, plucking away on his guitar. She turned back to Jack.

"No. Not tonight. But soon."

"That's cool," Jack said, unfazed. "What are you doing tomorrow?"

She ignored his question and got up and walked over to

the window that overlooked the alley below. She sat on the sill and put her head outside. She breathed in the fresh air. The room had gotten pretty smoky. Bart was sitting next to the window, and Nini began chatting with him, now ignoring Jack.

"I scraped my cylinder for the first time today. On the bay road," Nini boasted.

"That's so cool, Nini! You gotta be careful of the road-marker bumps though, you hit one of those with your cylinder and you'll flip."

"Totally," Nini said, smiling. She looked briefly over to Jack, who was watching them. He didn't really have anything else to do.

Bart smiled back at her, sensing her attraction to Jack.

"Remember when Blake crashed into that tree on that river run we did? He clipped a marker with his peg. Those things are death. He was laid up in your bed for like two weeks, wasn't he?

Nini smiled at Bart for trying scare off the wolves.

"Yeah. He was."

Bart passed her his cigarette, and she took a drag, watching Jack across the room as she blew out the smoke.

That night Nini and I rode home through dense fog. My headlight was on the fritz so she rode in front, and I followed her tail light closely. It was cold, and I had not worn a sweater under my leather jacket. We stopped on the top of a hill that often had a strange thermal pocket that trapped hot hair from the incoming marine layer that pushed inland from the coast in the evening. We shared a cigarette and warmed our hands over the hot cylinders of our bikes.

"You like him?"

She knew who I meant. She thought about it as she tugged on the smoke.

"Yeah. I don't want to, but I do."

"Because of Blake?"

"Yeah, just seems like too soon. He's still so hurt. I hate that he feels bad."

"You sure you don't want to get back together with him?"

"Yeah. I'm not in love with him anymore. I can't lie to myself or him. I love him, I always will, but I'm not in love with him."

"I get it," I said, and I did. He had been her first real boyfriend. It lasted over a year. But it had been marred by her fascination with Jerry. She had fucked it up, she knew it, and it had, in the end, led her to fall out of love with a man she otherwise might have stayed with into the foreseeable future. They had been a good couple. Their temperaments dovetailed well, both of them being understanding and calm, and he had been willing to try to understand her and her increasingly common bouts of deep sadness, even when he couldn't, which meant a lot to her. When she slept with Jerry, he didn't get angry. He was very sad, and didn't understand why she had done it, but he listened when she explained. I had listened too, to her explanation, and it made sense. But I was surprised that such a young man had taken it to heart, because it wasn't a mistake exactly that she described, it was a passion. She had felt such a passion for Jerry that she couldn't physically resist it. He had become, through his calm — almost laughably so — lack of pursuit, a prize too enticing to resist. Having him had become something of an obsession, one that she had kept hidden from those around her and even herself. When he returned from Baja, she realized she wanted him. More than anything, she wanted him inside her. She wanted to please him, and for him to please her. In her madness for him, she had hoped she could have him, just once, and never let Blake know. What he didn't know wouldn't hurt him, she thought. Of course she had been caught, and he did know, but even so her rationale had proven correct, for it was just that once that satiated her need for him, and she never slept with him again, remaining faithful to Blake until breaking up with him some months later. Blake had never retaliated, or even held it against her. After they patched things up he seemed to have forgotten all about it, and they had continued on as if it had never happened, going to school, planning for the future. It had been good. But it had not been enough. Nini began to chafe at his demands on her time. The hole of darkness she would descend into became more common during this period as well. Sometimes she didn't want to see Blake, sometimes she couldn't. Finally she had just ended it, summarizing her reason with, "I just need freedom." He cried for five hours. I could hear him wailing from inside the house the day she told him. He cried and cried, begging, pleading, becoming angry, screaming, crying again. But she was resolute, and that was the end. And after that five hours he accepted it.

"So what are you gonna do?" I asked as I stomped the butt out and climbed on my bike.

She thought for a long moment while pulling her helmet on. She looked at me with a look I could not read, then slapped the visor shut. Without another word she started her bike, and we rode off.

The next day she didn't come home from school until late at night. I heard her bike and got up and went to the window. She was alone, so I threw some clothes on and went out to her bus.

"So? Did you go to Jack's?"

She nodded as she pulled off her boots.

I waited for more.

"Got a smoke?"

"Not on me. You want me to go get one?"

She shook her head.

"No, I'm gonna go to sleep."

"Did you guys get together?"

"No."

"Do you like him?"

"Yes."

I waited for more. No more came. She climbed into bed. I walked to the door.

"Good night," I said as I stepped out.

"OK," was her only reply.

The next morning at breakfast, Nini was quiet. Our little sister was melting down over not having anything to wear so she and our mother went to her room, leaving Nini and me alone.

"What's wrong?" I asked.

She was quiet for a long moment, then looked at me.

"Do I look fat?" she asked, very matter of fact.

I looked her over. She wasn't skinny, she had always had curves, but she wasn't "fat" as I would think of it.

"No. Why?"

"I can tell Jack thinks I'm fat. He put his hands around my waist and his face changed. And we were alone in his room and he didn't try anything."

"That doesn't mean he thinks you're fat. Maybe he just takes things slow. You know, Sidney told me that guys always take it slow with the girls they like, the ones they want for girlfriends. If they know they don't want you around long term, they just try to fuck you," I said, agreeing. It made sense, somehow.

"I know that, I'm a girl."

"Well, I didn't know it."

She paused.

"Do you think it's true?" she asked, after careful consideration.

I thought about how Jerry had approached it, never making a move, teasing it out until she couldn't resist. I decided it was best not to bring him up.

"I don't know. But it's kinda like what used to happen to me. When I'd get that weird sister-feeling after sex."

"You don't get that anymore? Ever?"

I shook my head.

"No, but the point is that maybe guys do kinda know when the right girl comes along, or that at least sometimes it's better to get to know someone before having sex … ?"

She thought for a moment.

"Last weekend when that girl from Fairfax gave you a blowjob in the bathroom at Sidney's office, you didn't get that feeling?"

"No, but I told you, I never get it anymore. Not since it went away with Monica. I'm starting to think I was just too young to fuck. My body could do it, but my mind couldn't."

"Whatever, back to the girl in the bathroom. Did you think maybe you'd go out with her? Like, did you like her?"

"Not really. I thought she was pretty, and sexy, but it didn't really occur to me. Plus, she was all over me, so I didn't really have a chance." It was true, this girl had cornered me in the bathroom and just started grabbing me. I had of course obliged, but didn't get much thinking in during the episode.

"OK. I don't think this proves Jack doesn't think I'm fat."

Our mother came back into the room, and Nini got up and collected her things, then left for school.

That night she got home late again. I went to her bus.

"Did you go see Jack again?"

She nodded. A dark cloud hung over her head.

"How'd it go?"

"He thinks I'm fat."

"I told you, just because …"

"No, we had sex. He told me after he'd never had sex with a girl as fat as me but that he kind of liked it."

I was silent. What kind of asshole says something like that?

"I could tell the whole time. He kept avoiding putting his hands on my waist. He says I have love handles."

"What the fuck?"

"I asked him if he still liked my body even though I was fat. He said I'm not 'super fat,' just a 'little fat.' He said he likes my tits and my ass, but that for the right ratio my waist needs to be smaller."

"What a total asshole. Well, fuck him."

She was silent. I could tell this wasn't over.

"Did you tell him to fuck off?"

"No."

"Why not?"

"Because I really like him."

Nini and Jack began taking long rides together, exploring the California coast. He took her to Santa Cruz to meet some of his old friends. They rode north into Mendocino and camped for a weekend in a state park. They began to dress alike. Or Jack began to dress like Nini, anyway. He bought some heavy boots, a leather jacket. They looked like a couple. He seemed to worship her, but upon returning from their trips Nini would sink into depression, complaining that he was not satisfied by her or that he didn't like her body.

"But did he say your belly was hanging over your belt, or did you just feel like he thought that?" I asked as she lay on her bed after returning from a short trip they'd taken to Bolinas.

"I could see him looking."

"I think you're paranoid. He seems crazy about you."

"Well you're not there all the time. When we have sex he always keeps his hands away from my stomach, or my 'love handles.'"

"What does he do with them?"

"I don't know …" she said. After some thought, she continued. "Holds onto my ass if he's on top, or my tits if we're doing it doggy style. Most guys put their hands on your waist if they're coming from behind. He always holds my boobs or just dangles his arms at his sides, which is weird."

"Maybe he likes your boobs …? I do that sometimes."

"You don't hold a girl by her waist if you're doing it doggy style?"

"Sometimes, but not always," I said, thinking back to the handful of girls I had had sex with in that position. Monica and I had done it many times during the year or so that we went out, and I had recently become fond of it and moved to it quickly after the routine of beginning in missionary position.

Nini stood up and turned to a full-length mirror. She pulled her shirt off and looked at herself, now only in a bra and jeans.

"My hip-to-waist ratio sucks," she said, turning side to side. She wasn't shaped like an hour glass, but she never had been. I didn't understand why this preoccupation had become so central to her.

"Nini, you're crazy. Jack spends every free minute he has with you. He doesn't think you're fat."

"He told me I should stop washing my face with soap, that my skin would clear up."

I sighed. Damn this guy.

"Your skin is fine. So much better than it was."

Her acne was finally starting to go away. With a little make-up she was able to completely conceal it.

She leaned into the mirror and studied her skin. As she did, I looked her over. I thought she looked good. I thought Jack must be a real asshole to tell her these things. But I was confused by him. Whenever I was with them, he was really pretty great. He acted like she was everything to him. I liked him. I liked how he treated her. So what was the deal? She liked him, maybe even loved him, even though he made her feel like shit about her body. I couldn't square it.

"You want to go for a ride?" I asked, thinking it might pull her out of her funk.

"No. Let's get drunk," she said as she pulled a bottle of red wine out of her bag.

"OK."

I popped the cork as Nini changed into pajamas. I didn't feel like going into the house for glasses, so I grabbed a couple of teacups from a set she kept on a window sill and poured us a couple and we began to drink.

"I called dad last night," she said after a moment of silence.

"Yeah?"

She took another sip and thought about what to say. Finally, she just shrugged.

"What did he say?"

"He said he loved me."

"Huh. That's … cool."

She turned and looked at me without saying anything.

"Why'd you call him? Just to say hi?"

She finished her cup and poured another.

"I was missing him."

"Maybe we should ride up and see him one of these days."

"Maybe," she said, lighting a cigarette. "That's a fun ride anyway, through the redwoods."

I finished my glass, and she poured me another. We finished the bottle with some small talk and cigarettes. She put a record on her little turntable, and we sat silently listening to Loudon Wainright sing songs about his kids for a while until I fell asleep.

I awoke around midnight to find Nini was not there. I poked at her blankets to make sure she wasn't just buried under them. As I did, I noticed an old, tattered notebook sticking out from under a pillow. It was opened to a list of men's names. There were probably 40 or 50 names written in different inks, some in pencil. It seemed she had been keeping it for some time. The first name was Evan, then Bodi, then some names I didn't recognize, but it became obvious that it was a list of her lovers' names. I scanned it, recognizing some, not recognizing others. There was Dale Dork and Marcus, but who was Peter? And who was Stephan? And AJ? There was Blake and Jerry, followed by more names I didn't recognize, like Lief and Randy. Then there was Jack. But he was not the last name on the list. After Jack there was "James." Who was James? I didn't remember ever hanging out with a James. Maybe she met him at school? Maybe it was a long time ago and it was out of order? Was she sick of getting shit on by Jack and cheating on him? I slid the notebook back under her pillow.

I stepped out of the bus and looked over to the driveway. Her bike was there. I went into the house. She wasn't on the couch. I looked in my room, then my younger sister's. Finally I went to my mother's room. There was Nini, cuddled up to our mother in her pajamas. Mom's arms firmly around her. I stood and watched them sleep for a moment, then closed the door and went to bed.

Early the next morning I heard Nini's bike start and take off down the road. It was Friday, and we had plans to meet up in Petaluma, go to a concert at the Phoenix Theater, an old movie house that now had local bands play. I got up and had breakfast with my mother and younger sister.

"Nini slept with you last night?"

"It was so strange, she came in crying. I turned the light on, but she turned it back off, climbed in with me and cried for maybe 20 minutes and then fell asleep. She didn't want to talk, she just wanted to cry I guess," my mother said as she made a pot of tea.

"She's taking me for a ride to Point Reyes tomorrow," my little sister said. I noticed she had a hickey on her neck.

"What is that? Is that a hickey on your neck?" I said, excitedly.

She covered it with her hand.

"Who gave it to you?" I demanded.

She giggled and ran out of the room.

"Joel," my mother said. Joel was a kid my age from Point Reyes. He rode a motorcycle, too, but kept mostly to West Marin. I liked him alright, but was shocked my little sister was now entering into our dating pool. I knew she'd been asking Nini a lot of questions, and Nini had even started to take her on little trips into town. Sidney had fallen hard for her before being told not to touch her or Nini would castrate him. She wore a leather jacket, too, but was too young to drive or ride on her own.

"You know him?" my mother asked. Not because she was worried, but because she was curious.

"Yeah, he's cool. I just can't believe she's getting together with boys my age," I said. She chuckled.

"You guys are all so sex crazy. You know I was a virgin until I was 21."

"Twenty one?" I said in disbelief. "You didn't have sex with anyone until you were 21? No way."

She smiled and nodded.

DAVID.

I could hear the phone ringing from bed. I waited for someone else to pick it up, but no one did, so I got up and walked to the kitchen. The house was empty. I guessed my mother and stepfather had taken my little sister to school.

"Hello?"

I could hear only sniffling.

"Hello?"

More sniffling.

"Nini?"

"Yeah."

"What's wrong? Are you crying?"

More sniffling.

"Where are you?"

"I'm at Rod's house."

"Are you serious?"

"Yeah. He's in the shower."

"What the fuck are you doing at Rod's house?"

More sniffling and a long silence.

"Last night I ran into Mona at Kelly's house. We were talking, and we started talking about what a small town it is and how the dating pool is so small. And we started comparing notes. And it turned out we had a couple people in common, you know, that we had gotten together with. She got together with Rod a couple of times."

"Oh," I said. Yeah, no shit.

"And I started talking about how he couldn't get it up for anything but a blowjob. And she was looking at me really weird, so I asked her if it was the same with her and she said no, she had never given him a blowjob, but that he wasn't very good in bed, came way too fast and always wanted to leave right after."

"I'm not surprised."

More silence, more sniffling.

"It was just me. He didn't want to have sex with me. He just wanted me to give him head."

Now I was silent for a minute.

"It was just me."

"I get it … . So what are you doing at his house?"

Silence.

"I mean, how'd you wind up at his house?"

"I was hanging out in front of the Western, after Mona left, and he showed up."

"He just showed up?"

"I called him. And he came."

"Oh."

"And we went to his house. I wanted to see if he would have sex with me. We kissed … it was really nice. I really missed him I guess."

"Been a while."

"Yeah. So we kissed, then he unzipped his fly. I told him I didn't want to give him head. I wanted to have sex."

"And? What did he do?"

"He said it was that or nothing."

I took a long breath.

"So what did you do?"

"I gave him head."

We both sat there, saying nothing for a long time. I heard her sniffle a little more.

"He's out of the shower. I have to go."

A few hours later I heard Nini's bike pull up, so I went out to greet her. She just sat on her bike as I approached, letting it idle.

"I was starting to wonder if you were OK."

She took her helmet off. Her face was streaked with tears.

"Are you OK?"

She killed the bike's engine and took a halting deep breath. I readied myself for the full lowdown on Rod.

"On the way home there was a crash. I was the first one there."

I waited. Someone we knew? I waited.

"David Shorestein."

"Is he OK?"

She shook her head.

"He was lying on the ground. He got thrown out of the car. He was still breathing when I got there. But he stopped. I was with him when he stopped breathing."

I took a deep breath and held the tears in. David was a kid we knew from a town over. Not a good friend, but one of us. Our parents knew each other. He was an only child. I had always thought he was cool. He played guitar and kept to himself. He was a couple of years older than Nini and didn't really hang out with our crowd. But he was one of us, and now he was gone.

Nini got off her bike, and I followed her into her bus, where she fell face down on her bed and began to sob. I sat and watched her for a while, then went into the house. I told my mom, who began to cry. She and I went back out to the bus and sat with Nini as she sobbed. Our mother sang. Not a song, no words, just her voice, singing an unrecognizable melody. Finally Nini looked up. She looked at me for a long time, then she and I listened as our mother sang.

CHARLES.

The Phoenix was jumping. A large crowd was gathered outside the box office. Nini and Bart were sitting on their bikes at the curb, talking. I pulled up beside them. As I backed it in I noticed a pretty girl with large blonde ringlets watching me. She wore jeans with holes in the knees, Doc Martin boots and a leather jacket. I pretended she wasn't there.

"We were starting to think you weren't coming," Bart said, pulling on his ever-present cigarette.

"I stopped for gas, and my bike wouldn't start again. I kicked and kicked, I pushed it, it wouldn't fire. Finally I realized that my plug wires were off, some fucker had pulled them when I went in to pay."

Bart smiled but said nothing. Nini smiled, too.

"You fuckers! It took me like half an hour to figure it out."

"You shouldn't have talked to the girl behind the cash register for so long," Nini said between laughs.

"You guys suck," I said as I swung my leg over my bike and walked over to the doors to have a look inside. It was packed. I walked back over and as I did, the blonde girl stepped up beside me.

"I like your bike," she said. Her voice was very soft and quiet, and it broke just a tiny bit.

I was in love. I just knew it the moment she spoke. Her voice flooded over me like water in a warm bath.

"What's your name?"

"Nora. My mom and dad ride old bikes, too."

"Yeah? That's cool. You like to ride?"

She nodded silently. We looked at each other for a long time. She swayed a little, smiled a little. Each breath I took lasted an hour. She blinked in slow motion. Finally I said the only thing I could think of.

"You want to go for a ride?"

"OK."

I led her over to my bike.

"We're going for a ride," I said to Nini and Bart. I could tell they were impressed. I climbed on and kicked it over.

"Hop on," I said, and Nora climbed on the back. She put her arms around my waist, naturally and without reservation. I shared a quick glance with Nini. She squinted at me, letting me know she knew what I was saying: "Holy shit, I'm so fucking lucky. I'm madly in love with this girl and I just met her."

Nora and I rode around town a bit. She held tight and knew how to lean into corners. Her warm legs pressed hard against my thighs. She spoke into my ear, not yelling, but getting very close and speaking in her quiet soft way, her lips pressed against me.

"Let's go faster."

I steered us out of town and into the countryside. I opened it up, and we sped through the sweeping curves that led out of town. She held me tighter, her soft cheek cradled in my neck. A few miles out I pulled the bike over under a street light. I killed it, and we climbed off.

"That's so fun!" she said, giddy with excitement.

Then she calmed. She looked up at me with her big blue eyes, tears still welled in them from the wind.

We kissed. More hot water in the bath. It was real. I could tell she was in the bath, too. This was real.

We pulled up at the Phoenix, and I parked the bike between Nini and Bart's bikes and another bike I didn't recognize. It was a newer bike, and it was red, a color we frowned upon as "too showy." Nora hopped off as if she had hopped off my bike a thousand times. She grabbed my hand, and we walked up to the ticket window.

Inside I looked for Nini. We walked upstairs, and I found her leaning against the doorjamb of the balcony, watching the band. She looked us over, holding hands, and smiled. She and Nora shared a glance. Nora waited for approval. Nini approved and Nora smiled back.

"Where's Bart?" I asked.

"Down in the front."

I spotted Jack across the balcony, heading down the stairs on the other side of the bannister. He was with a bespectacled girl with bleach-blonde hair. He looked up at me just before they disappeared into the lobby below. I turned to Nini.

"Did you talk to him?"

She nodded.

"Who's he with?"

"Her name's Claude or something."

"You OK? What's the deal?"

She nodded, thought for a moment and nodded again.

"Yeah. Now I'm sure."

I hadn't seen Jack around for a couple of weeks, but we hadn't talked about it. Whenever I'd asked about him, she had changed the subject.

"You guys want to go down?" I asked them both.

"You go. I want to watch from up here."

"Why?" I asked. It was a weird place to watch from. "Fuck him. Fuck them."

"Hi, I'm Charles," a straight-looking dude in his early 20s with big teeth and clean brown hair said as he stepped up to us from the bathroom, which was a few feet away. He was tall, dressed in khaki pants and an oxford shirt. He held a brown bomber jacket in one hand and a motorcycle helmet in the other.

"This is my brother and …?"

"Nora."

"This is Charles," Nini said, then looked at me for my reaction.

"Hi, Charles."

"Nini has told me a lot about you," Charles said in a friendly way. But I didn't like him. I wasn't exactly sure why, but his big teeth and clean, collared shirt bothered me.

"Cool. Glad to hear she still likes me."

"I didn't say that she liked you, just told me a lot about you …" he said with a toothy grin. I disliked him even more.

"OK."

We stood there for an awkward moment. Charles looked at Nini for guidance. Nini and I looked at each other. I tilted my head just a bit, as if to say, "He's a dick." She raised her eyebrows just enough to say, "I don't care."

"Well, we're gonna go down and watch the band," I said, then led Nora towards the stairs.

We found Bart near the stage. He was rocking his head to the beat. He looked over at us, saw our handholding and nodded to me, then looked back up at the band with a little smile on his face. Bart always felt a certain pride when I managed to get together with a girl, and he always let me know it. He had great confidence in my nascent powers of seduction, and I think he got a little charge out of each one of my conquests — as if we were on the same team, and any score was a score for the team. We would scope out girls together and he would insist, "You could get her." He was the perfect wingman; filling me with confidence but never pursuing the same girls I set my sights on.

After the show, Nora found her friends and went home after a spectacular scene in which she turned from her friends and ran back into my arms for a final kiss of the night.

Bart and I waited by our bikes for Nini. As the last of the kids filed out of the theater, Nini and Charles strolled out, his arm draped over her shoulder. Bart looked him over with disdain.

"Where's the girl?" Nini asked. There was just a hint of a challenge in her question. She could tell we didn't approve of Charles, and she was feeling defiant.

"She went home. I got her number."

"You see Charles' bike?"

"Yeah."

We all looked over to Charles' red Ducati. New. Expensive.

"Nice bike," I said.

"You want to take it for a spin?" Charles asked, earnestly. He was trying.

"No, I'm good. I like my bike."

Charles smiled and shrugged. Nini looked at me and shook her head.

"Asshole," her eyes said.

"You going to Sidney's, Nini?" Bart asked.

"Yeah, but we're going to get a drink first," she replied, then looked at me.

"A drink? Where are you going to get a drink?" I said,

incredulously. She wasn't 21, and we had long ago given up trying to sneak into any bars in town.

"Charles' friend works at McBeers," she said.

McBeers was just the kind of place Charles would go, I thought. It was a sports bar that sold "wings" and that sort of thing. There were TVs and thick-necked assholes everywhere.

"McBeer's?" Bart asked, a sneer on his face. Then he shrugged, and the sneer disappeared. He smiled at Nini. "Well, hopefully we'll see you at Sidney's after?" We had open disgust for anyone who went to McBeer's, but Bart's affection for Nini trumped it. She didn't notice, however, and I could tell it bummed her out that we weren't more supportive.

"Probably," Nini said, putting her helmet on.

Bart and I rode over to Sidney's office. I could think only of Nora.

Sidney's was in full swing. A bunch of kids from the show at the Phoenix were there. It was always exciting when kids from out of town came to Sidney's. New blood. There was the girl from Fairfax there who had given me a blowjob in the bathroom a couple of weeks before. She looked beautiful in a short strapless green-velvet dress and big black shoes with silver buckles. Her big brown eyes flared when she smiled at me. We had only just met when she asked me to go to the bathroom with her the week before. She had been watching me from across the room while I chatted with her friend and then had abruptly interrupted us and asked me to follow her. I did. Once in the bathroom she had attacked me, kissing me briefly and then unzipping my pants. When she was done, we went back and she talked to the same friend, ignoring me. I couldn't remember her name.

Now she looked at me from across the room again as Bart and I entered the office. I pretended not to see her. My heart was locked down. Nora occupied my every thought. I imagined her face, the sun behind it filtering through her long blonde ringlets, her generous, soft lips smiling at me. The girl from Fairfax walked over.

"Aren't you going to say hi?" she asked, then looked at me with coy eyes.

"Yeah, we just got here."

"We didn't get a chance to talk much last time I saw you."

"Yeah …"

"Kinda had my mouth full," she smiled. Bart rolled his eyes and walked over to Blake, who was playing guitar by himself. I had filled Bart in after the party the previous week, so he knew the score. The girl looked up at me, waiting for a move. But I wasn't into it. Nora … Nora … Nora …

"Got a smoke?" I asked her, unable to think of anything else.

She shook her head.

"I quit. You should, too."

"Yeah …"

I walked over to Bart and asked him for a smoke. I had a pack in my pocket but now felt like it would be too cruel to reveal it. Bart gave me a smoke and lit it for me.

"I think I'm gonna head home."

"With her?" Bart asked, motioning to the girl from Fairfax.

"No, I'm tired. Just gonna head home and go to bed."

Brad looked at me, studying my face for a clue. He knew that I would never normally pass on a sure thing with a girl so good-looking and so willing. After a moment he realized.

"Oh … that blonde girl."

"Yeah. Nora."

"I get it. Keep the shiny side up."

I said goodbye to a couple of more people, then walked to the door, where the girl was waiting for me.

"Leaving already?"

"Yeah, I gotta get home."

"Whatever," she said, looking at me like I was abandoning her.

I started to walk out the door, but she stayed with me.

"Don't you think we have some unfinished business?" she said as I started down the stairs.

"Seems like we finished it."

"So you think a girl just sucks your dick, and that's all she wants?"

"No …" Fuck, I didn't know. She had just done it. I didn't ask for it. Many times I had, but not this time. It was a freebie as far as I knew.

"How about you give me some head? Same same. Quid pro quo." I had heard this term before. Sidney liked to sprinkle his monologues with Latin, but I didn't know what it meant.

We got to the gate. I was just about to open it when I looked out and realized there was a giant brawl, almost a riot, occurring right outside of the metal gate, in the street. Sidney's office was located downtown, in what people of an older generation called the "herpes triangle." Three bars on two parallel streets that got really rowdy on the weekends. A mix of cowboys, jocks, bikers, weekend warriors and the ladies who dressed up for them would often find a reason for "go time." The fights often spread into the street, but nothing like this. There were at least 75 people kicking the shit out of each other in the middle of the street. Kicking and punching, rolling around in the gutter. The girl from Fairfax and I stopped and watched silently through the bars of the gate. A young guy with a mullet got slammed against the gate, and we jumped back.

"Help," he said. "Let me in." We did not. His attacker was an enormous jock with a softball jersey on. The guy with the mullet was dragged down the street, out of sight. I spotted Nini and Charles. They were running along the building, trying to stay out of sight. I waited until they had just reached the gate before opening it. They swept in, and I slammed it shut as two biker-looking dudes rushed it. The four of us retreated up a few steps.

"What the fuck?" I said to anyone who might have an answer.

"It started in McBeer's, over a baseball game or something, but I guess someone called Andersen's and it started there, too," Charles said.

The girl from Fairfax ran upstairs to tattle.

"You got in, huh?" I asked Nini.

"Yep. Didn't even get carded," she said with a smirk.

"Cool."

Sidney and a bunch of others came down the steps to watch the brawl. All of our bikes, which were lined up at the curb just in front of the gate, were miraculously spared any kicking or knocking over, though at one point a guy with a particularly bloody face hid behind them after getting kicked in the face by a baseball jersey-wearing jock.

After a few minutes of fighting, the cops showed up and began arresting people. I decided it was better to hang for a while than go out and get caught up in the mess.

Nini, the girl from Fairfax whose name I still did not know, Charles and I sat together near the window. Nini was smoking. The girl partially hung her head out the window, theatrically trying to avoid the smoke, but we all ignored it.

"So what's your deal, Charles?" the girl from Fairfax asked as she played footsie with him.

"My deal?"

"What do you do? What are you into?" she asked,

squinting her eyes and trying to look really interested. Charles wasn't into it, either.

"Right now I'm pretty into the girl I came with," he said, letting it sink in.

Kudos, I thought. Then I figured he probably got a lot of that. He was tall, really good looking — like an underwear model — and had that blue-blood kind of thing about him. He was scrubbed. He looked rich.

"Whatever," said the girl from Fairfax. She looked at Nini as she began to get up.

"Is Petaluma just full of fags or what?" She walked out into the hall.

"Fags? Didn't she give you a blowjob in the bathroom?" Nini asked.

"Yeah, a good one, too," I replied, feeling a little guilty. She was lonely, the girl from Fairfax. Why else would she come so far to try to find someone to mess around with? And now she was getting kind of desperate. I knew the feeling. Many a time had I looked around at the end of the night, seeking vainly the girl who might still be willing ...

"I'm going to check if it's clear yet. We should get on the road," Charles said as he got up. I saw Blake across the room, trying in vain not to give Charles the once-over, which he finally did, then turned in disgust.

"OK," Nini said, smiling up at him from her seat on the floor.

Once he was gone, Nini turned to me.

"You're not into her? She's cute. She's totally into you. She was doing that to make you jealous, you know that right?"

It hadn't occurred to me, but now I saw that she was probably right. It didn't matter though.

"It doesn't matter. I'm in love."

"With the blonde girl?"

"Yeah. Really in love. I can't think of anything else. Seriously, from the first time I saw her face, I was totally in love with her."

"Wow. Love at first sight. Never happened to me like that. At least no one ever told me if it did." She thought about it for a moment.

"It probably did, and no one told you," I said, trying to make her feel better.

"Maybe."

"So, what's up with Charles?

"Charles is just a friend."

"Have you slept with him?"

"No, but I might. But we're just friends. I know I don't love him. He's too … he's too much."

Charles had returned to the room and was chatting with Sidney about a painting on the wall — of a woman's legs — that Sidney had recently painted, but he couldn't keep his eyes off of Nini, they were pulled back every time he looked away. He couldn't stop taking her in, looking her over, looking for whatever it was that he found compelling about her. Because it wasn't obvious. He could have any woman. But he wanted her. He didn't know why, but he was searching for it. He watched her laugh, he looked her body over. He stared at her boobs, her belly.

Nini and I did the same to him.

"Look at him. Everything is too much about him. He's too tall, he's got too many bones in his face. He's got too many teeth, and they're too big," Nini said, quietly and discreetly.

I looked him over. I agreed, but still, he was what most men aspired to. It made me feel good that Nini found it "too much."

"I bet he's good in bed," I said, and we both laughed.

"Yeah. I bet you're right. And rich."

We laughed again.

"He kissed me at McBeer's. I was kind of surprised that he'd kiss me in public. He tasted like chicken.

We busted up again.

"So, what about Jack? You guys are done?"

"He makes me sad. I love him, but he makes me sad. I can't be with him anymore."

"So that chick is his new girlfriend?"

"I guess so."

"Did you guys even break up? Did you ever talk? He just kinda disappeared."

"Yeah. I told him. He cried. You ever hear of make-up sex? Well there's break-up sex, too. So we had sex, and then I left and now we're done."

"You feel better?"

"No. I feel sad."

"About the girl?"

"No. Just about Jack."

"Maybe fucking Mr. Too Much will make you feel better," I said.

She smiled. But it was a sad smile. A regretful smile.

"Yeah, maybe it will … . But it won't matter."

"Nothing matters," I said, feeling existential, a notion I had recently heard of from Sidney, but only vaguely understood.

"Some things matter," Nini said with a sigh.

"What?"

"Love."

"What about sex?"

She thought about this for a moment.

"Sometimes sex matters."

"When does sex matter?" Charles said as he dropped down beside Nini. She looked him over.

"When you can't get it," Sidney said, dropping in beside

me. He earned a little chuckle from Charles.

"Does sex have meaning?" Charles asked, trying to seem groovy. I figured he must have been taking a philosophy course or something. Nevertheless, I was impressed with us, that we were having such a philosophical conversation, even a shallow one.

"Only love has meaning. Sex means nothing unless you're in love. It's just for kicks," I said, feeling adventurous and in love.

"Everyone knows sex is better when you're in love … right?" said Sidney.

I looked at Nini. She was looking out the window, into the darkness. I wondered what sex really meant to her. She had had so much of it. Did it mean anything?

Nini, Charles and I rode home together. It was a clear night, with no fog, and we rode fast and smooth, all in a single-file line — Nini in front, then Charles, then me. We didn't plan it, it just happened that way. Nini had gotten out in front and stayed there. As we leaned through the curves, I watched Nini's tiny body perched on her big bike, leading us through the night. She seemed fearless. She set the pace fast and kept at it, leaning into each curve perfectly, tilting her head to level, searching for the line through the curve. I watched Charles, too, following her every move, chasing her through the dark. She would never love him. I didn't know if that was even what he wanted. He saw her, though; he saw Nini and was drawn to her. I could see that in the way he looked at her. He loved her. He wasn't in love with her, but her warmth and friendliness had infected him with a need to be around her, just like it had so many others. I was glad for her, watching her up there in front, alone, battling the darkness with her headlight, foot by foot, leaning back and forth through the night for miles. What was she speeding toward? I had always thought it was sex she wanted, good sex, better than the last sex. But now, watching her, I knew it wasn't, and she knew it, too, maybe for the first time. Sex was right behind her, chasing her through the night. But she wasn't slowing down for it, she was gunning it, full speed into the darkness. She was hunting for something. Hoping it would be there, around the next curve, in the next foot of road. What was it? For the first time, my naïve mind stumbled upon the truth about my sister. My fearless sister was searching for love. Real and total love. Not love that made her sad, or wanting someone else. Love that consumed her. Something I knew she had never had.

When we got home, I said good night to Charles and Nini, and watched them go into her bus. Then I went into my room and got in bed. A few minutes later I heard Charles' bike start, and he rode away. She had turned him away. Well done, I thought. Sometimes too much is not enough. I went to sleep.

HEATH.

Nini dropped her bike. I jumped off my bike and ran over to her, helping her to lean the big BMW back up and put it on its kickstand. We'd been through this routine countless times. She couldn't touch the ground on both sides at the same time, so if the ground was uneven and too low on one side, she'd go down. We steadied the bike, and she climbed back on. She had long lost any embarrassment associated with dropping the bike, but it did become problematic if there was no one around to help her right it. Somehow she always managed. She smiled at me in thanks, and I jumped back on my bike and kicked it over. We rode north through Valley Ford, then through Freestone and into the redwoods. We stopped for gas in Occidental, then continued up the hill, finally pulling off the road onto a little dirt driveway. I gunned it, kicking some rocks at Nini, who flipped me off, then pulled in front of me and did the same, hitting me in the face with some small pebbles. We pulled up to a little house nestled in the woods. We revved the bikes a couple of times, and then killed them. As we dismounted, our father emerged from the house, wiping his hands with a paint-splattered rag.

"Jesus you guys, those bikes are so loud," he said as he hugged each one of us.

"I just put straight pipes on mine," I said proudly.

"My turpentine cans were all rattling like there was an earthquake," he said with a chuckle. His long hair fell into his face a bit. He pushed it back, revealing his receding hairline. I noticed there was more gray than there was the last time I'd seen him, which was a few months before. His thick glasses reflected the canopy of redwoods above us as his head tilted back. He wiped his hands on his paint-covered apron and looked us each over.

"So ..." He took a long pause.

"We just thought we'd stop by, say hello," Nini said, intuiting what was coming next.

"Yeah, I wasn't expecting you."

"Are you busy?" I asked.

"I'm right in the middle of a painting ..." he said, knowing he would disappoint us. "You know it's always best if you give me a little warning. That way I can be ready ... I won't be right in the middle of something."

"Can you take a little break? We can't stay long anyway," Nini said, disregarding his request.

He thought for a moment. I could feel his body being pulled back into the house. He was fighting it. He studied Nini's face. She stared back at him, intently. She wasn't testing, she just wanted him to know it was important.

"Yeah. I can take a little break. I was just going to have a beer anyway," he said finally. "Why don't you guys have a seat. I'll just clean up a bit and grab a beer, and I'll be right back."

Nini and I took a seat on a couple of wooden chairs and watched him rush back into the house.

"Seems like he's home alone," I said, looking over to

where his girlfriend usually parked her car.

"Yeah. I think it makes him nervous to have people over when she's not home," Nini responded.

"Maybe 'cause it's her house?" I wondered aloud.

After a few minutes he came back out. The apron was gone, and he had a beer in his hand.

"I'd offer you a beer, but I'd hate to see you ride those things with a buzz," he said. Then he took a big swig. He sat across from us awkwardly, as if being interviewed. I knew quite the opposite would soon unfold.

"It's fine. I never drink when I ride," Nini said. I nodded in agreement.

"So ..." he began again, taking a long pause. He studied us each for a long moment, then zeroed in on Nini. I sighed with relief, under my breath, knowing that there was little chance we'd get to me.

"It's been a little while." There was a musicality to his speech when he began a conversation. The beats and pauses marking his thoughts as he formulated an approach.

"How's your writing?" "Are you writing?" "Is it good?" "Is it fulfilling you?"

"It's good." "Yeah, I am." "I don't know." "No, I'm not fulfilled." Nini's replies came staccato, dry. She began to squirm in her seat as his probing mind began to build the arena in which they would now parry. She knew there was no reason to sugarcoat anything. He would ask the questions, and he would get the truth.

"Why aren't you fulfilled?" "How's your love life?" "Are you seeing someone?" He dug, drawing her in.

"I don't know." "I don't have one." "Yes." She answered. This piqued his interest.

"You don't have a love life, but you are seeing someone?" he said, then took a long swig from his beer. I waited for the answer.

"Yeah."

Nini had been seeing a guy named Heath who worked at the café in Petaluma as a dishwasher. He was a strange guy, in his early 20s. His head was shaved, and he looked like a monk. This didn't seem to be an accident, because he also acted like one. He was calm and quiet, usually only speaking when spoken to. He had a small, perpetual smile on his face, as if his lips were stuck in that happy place permanently. His glass-like eyes were wide and open, and he seemed like a genuine seeker type. Not a hippie, but a seeker, someone who was looking for the truth, whatever that meant. This was not my observation. Nini had explained it to me after their first date, which was a walk they took one evening after he got off work. They had sparked a pleasant repartee as he occasionally came out to pick up the dirty dishes off the tables. Usually someone would ask his opinion on the current subject of conversation, and he would reply with an earthy observation he had made about human nature. Always with positivity. It was this positivity that had drawn Nini to him. After a few weeks Nini asked him if he wanted to hang out, and he offered a walk as a possibility. Bart and I watched from our seats at the café as they walked up the hill towards the big Catholic church. I'd kept my eye on them as he gesticulated to the towers of the church and Nini nodded along, seeming very interested in what he was saying about them. Since then they had begun taking increasingly longer walks together and had even taken a trip to the city together, where they walked across the Golden Gate Bridge.

"She's seeing a guy named 'Heath,'" I said, pronouncing it like the first syllable of "Heather."

"Heath?" our dad said, also pronouncing that way.

"Like 'Heath,'" Nini responded, now pronouncing it like most people would. "But he pronounces it 'Heath,'" she said, now saying it the awkward way.

Dad thought about this for a moment. He rolled it around in his mouth, then said it again, slowly. "Heath. Like Hef. But Heath."

Nini nodded.

"It's very awkward to say," he continued.

"It's very 'him,'" I said.

Nini shot me a glance.

"What? It is. He's a strange guy."

Nini shrugged.

"So …" Dad began again. "I'm curious why you are unfulfilled? Are you in love?"

Nini thought for a long moment. I could tell she didn't really want to get into this, but eventually he'd pry it out of her one way or another, so she capitulated.

"Heath doesn't believe in sex," she said, then waited.

He squinted as he mulled this over. He finished his beer. We both waited impatiently as he took his time to respond.

"Love without sex is brotherly love." He raised his eyebrows and looked at me, waiting for me to nod and acknowledge his profundity. I finally nodded, and he looked back to Nini. "From what you've told me in the past, Nini, you are a sexual being." He let that sink in for a moment, then stood up. "I have to get another beer."

Nini and I didn't look at each other for a moment as he disappeared into the house, then I finally turned to her.

"We could just get on our bikes and split before he comes back."

She shook her head. "No, I want to hear what he has to say."

"Are you serious about 'Heath'?"

She turned to me. "Serious that he doesn't believe in sex or serious about being with him?"

"Both."

"Yes. To both."

I was stunned. Who would consider a monogamous relationship with someone who didn't put out? Not Nini, surely.

"Seriously?"

She nodded as dad came out with another beer. He sat down and took a long swig. Then he looked at Nini for a long time.

"So … I had to pee when I went inside, and while I was peeing I thought a lot about what you've revealed to me so far about 'Heath.' Have you written about it?" he asked her.

"Yes."

"I know that when you tell me you've written about something, you've really examined your feelings and written them down. I know because when you've had me read your pages, I've seen it. You have an uncanny ability to examine your own feelings. And I think you are working them out in your writing. Am I wrong?"

She looked down and slowly shook her head "no."

I wondered what pages he was talking about. I had not read them. What did he know that I didn't? She trusted him to read them?

"Read it. Don't just write it. Go back, read it. And I think the answer to the questions you're asking yourself are in those pages."

I looked at Nini. Her eyes were glassy, but she didn't cry. She was communing with him. He was giving her what she had come for. It was simple, and it seemed like she would have probably figured it out for herself in the end, but he had just communicated to her in a fatherly way, at least in his fatherly way, and she was touched.

We rode home slowly, banking softly through the turns. When we got to the Valley Ford turnoff, Nini pulled off to the side of the road.

"I'm gonna go see Heath," she said, then flipped her visor down. I nodded and watched her ride off until she was just a black dot that disappeared over a rise in the road.

"I kissed him. He kissed me back. We went to his apartment. I didn't realize he lives right above the café. It's almost totally empty. He has like, a little cot and a lamp, and a stack of books. He stacks his books up like a tower after he reads them. The stack is taller than he is." Nini recalled all of this in a soft, wistful voice. She had come to my room as soon as she got home, so I knew something had happened that she wanted to share.

"What happened at his apartment?" I asked, wanting to get to the point.

"I kissed him again. I took off my clothes, and I asked him if he would sleep with me. He said, 'No.'"

I waited for more. She didn't continue.

"What kind of books does he read?" I asked, genuinely curious where he was getting these ideas about sex. I waited to hear about the philosophy, religion and political books he must read, this deep thinker who Nini was dealing with.

"Stephen King. Anne Rice. Horror. He loves horror."

I was shocked.

"Like, 'The Shining'? Stuff like that?"

"Yeah, it's one of his favorite books."

"That's so weird. So he's a celibate horror freak?"

"I wouldn't reduce him to that. But yeah," she said as she pulled a notebook from the small green army bag she had recently found at the Goodwill store, which was still slung over her shoulder. She opened the notebook, turned it to a page in the middle and handed it to me. I read the page:

"Deeply

I want to feel you

Deeply

Let me know your
Essence
Allow me to see
Inside
And throw the
Outside away
Allow me to trust
Completely
But not lose
Myself in you
Let's just be
Let my happiness
Be shared with you
I shall be complete."
I looked back up to her.
"I was wrong," she said, her voice cracking a little bit.
"Was it for him?" I asked.
She nodded. "I wrote it after our first walk together. I went to the café and read it over and over again. I wanted to be sure I meant it. That it was really how I feel. I let him read it. After he did he looked at me for like, two minutes. He just stared at me. I was naked. I had just read him that poem. I stood there like a total asshole. Finally, he asked me if I wanted to get a cup of coffee."
"Why do you like him?"
She thought for a moment.
"He's different … he's always happy. He always has this blissed-out quality, like nothing can touch him. I want to be like that."
"Do you think sleeping with him will make you more like him?"
She didn't answer for a long time.
"He says he believes in God. And reincarnation. He says that we are all God. Part of God. He says sex with

me would dilute his connection to God. He says he really believes that. He believes celibacy is godlike. Or, as he put it, he believes cleanliness is next to godliness."

"Do you?" I asked, knowing the answer.

"No. Sex isn't dirty. Fuck him."

LOGAN.

I awoke with a start and looked out the window. I looked, but all I could see was Nora's face staring back at me, the sun filtering through her blonde ringlets. Her soft lips parted in an almost-smile that made her blue eyes squint just so. I lit a cigarette and tried to think of something else.

Bart and I made a pot of coffee and walked it over to Nini and Franny's small apartment behind our house. It was a large old Victorian that was rundown and carved up but still had plenty of charm. The four of us drank coffee and chatted about going for a ride out to the coast.

Bart and I had found the place first, but upon helping us move in, Nini and Franny discovered the back apartment was for rent as well. We were happy to have them back there. Bart and Franny struck up a once-in-a-while fling, and we could always go over and eat at their place if we ran out of food. I was nursing a broken heart after Nora had, six months in, suddenly revealed that she didn't love me anymore. It had been my first taste of mad, passionate love, and I had assumed it would go on indefinitely. After waiting two painful days to call her after our first kiss, she had come to the house and stayed the night. Nini was away with Franny and had offered her bus so I'd have some privacy. Nora and I had made a fire and kissed for hours before she took her clothes off and we did what I liked to think of as "making love." It sounded corny even just rattling around in my head, but I wanted to differentiate it from normal sex, so I settled on thinking of it that way. This was more. I felt more. It seemed like she did, too. When we awoke in the morning, the sun shone in on her pale, alabaster skin, and her soft, blonde ringlets blended into Nini's overstuffed white comforter to create a cloud-like, heavenly scene. We "made love" again in Nini's bed. I thought to myself that for perhaps the first time in my life there was absolutely nowhere I'd rather be. This was exactly what I wanted, nothing could have made me happier. That feeling lasted — for me — every time I was with Nora, for six months. I was thoroughly infatuated with her and instigated "lovemaking" in every available moment. I hadn't noticed the signs of her growing bored by my insatiable need for her. One day, sitting on a park bench, she broke the news to me. A crushing blow that I had not recovered from. I saw her softly lit face gazing out at me, the sun blazing behind her and filtering through her hair, wherever I looked. It was burned into my retinas. Lovely, heavenly … like that first morning. I dreamed it, waking or asleep. I couldn't escape it.

Nini had helped on the particularly lonely nights. Nini wasn't seeing anyone either, so we often drank and smoked into the early hours of the morning. She would read poems to me or comically trash Nora, always with a wink. I would laugh along, burning inside, but still, it helped. At least in the moment. Nini's love would warm me, and the icy wind of Nora's absence would recede, at least as long as Nini was awake. After she would go back to her apartment or pass out on the couch, I would rot, lying awake for hours, Nora's glowing face beckoning me with the promise of light but delivering only darkness.

Recently, Monica had visited Nini, and this led to us briefly rekindling our romance. Ours had begun in convenience and grown to a real love, but not of the crazy, lustful, do-or-die variety I had experienced with Nora. It was comforting to lie with her again. Our bodies fit together well, and it was such a familiar feeling to be inside her, I couldn't help but think of the possibilities. But it was not to be. Monica and I had grown so close during our relationship, and we were so young during it, that it had become, ironically, more like that of siblings, and like most siblings, we fought. Still, when she did come around, the animal attraction was strong enough that she would usually end up in my bed, and for a brief moment, until the sex was over, I could get Nora off of my mind.

"Do you remember Logan?" Franny asked me, then ignored a feigned glare from Nini.

"Yeah."

Franny smiled and sat back. She laughed a brief, hiccup of a laugh.

"He's in Nini's room."

Why she thought this funny, I didn't know. It was interesting, not funny, but Franny laughed easily. It was something everyone liked about her.

"Yeah?" I said, to Nini.

She smiled a broad, long smile and nodded.

"He came into my work."

"Cool."

Nini's room was only a few feet away, and the door was slightly ajar, so I felt uncomfortable talking about him.

There was silence for a moment, then Bart stood up.

"Well, are we gonna go for a ride or what?"

"I want to," Franny said.

"I'm in," I said, then looked to Nini for an answer.

"Yeah," she said. "Once Logan wakes up."

I kicked my bike over and let it warm up. Nini came out and started her bike, too. We spoke over the rumbling idle.

"You like him?"

"I cried."

"You cried? Why?"

"When we had sex."

"I'm sorry. Was he a dick?"

"No. He was … our souls touched. I don't even believe we have souls, but if we do … that's what if feels like. When he came in to work, the second I saw him I felt like his eyes saw right into me. I hadn't seen him in like, four years? He lives in L.A. He's up visiting his sister. You remember Myra?"

"Oh, yeah. I always wanted to fuck her."

"Everybody did."

"And everybody did."

"Yeah. We talked for like two minutes, and I thought of the way you described the first time you saw Nora. Love at first sight. I could see him seeing me that way, and I felt the same. It felt so good."

I thought back to the night at Mike's warehouse, when he had watched her so intently. Had he fallen in love with her right then and waited all this time to act on it?

"Except you already knew him."

"Yeah, but it was like seeing him for the first time. We could have kissed right there, he told me he totally felt it too. I left work early, and we came back and talked, and then we just had the most amazing experience …"

"You had sex?"

"Yeah, but it wasn't like sex that I've had before. It was like …"

"Making love?"

"That sounds so corny."

"I know, but it's pretty accurate, right?"

"Yeah. I guess so …" she said, contemplating it. "And he loves my body. He held me like no one else has ever held me. He kissed, and basically licked, like every inch of my body. For like an hour. It was like he was studying it. Just taking it in. And that was before we even did it. And then that was like a whole other thing. It made me believe for the first time that there may actually be one person out there for each of us. I think I found the one person in the world that is really, truly for me."

"Wow," I said, wondering how Logan felt about this. "That's awesome!"

She smiled as Logan stepped out of the house. He was as I remembered him — light-brown curly hair, slender and tan. His sparkly but narrowly set blue eyes twinkled with a friendliness I had rarely encountered before, and I could see how Nini had fallen so hard, so quickly. I had only ever spent a few hours with him, but I immediately wanted to spend more. He spoke with a soft, encouraging tone and moved slowly and deliberately, with no menace or bravado. It was like he asked permission with his eyes and body language before entering your space.

"Hey, dude," he said, and smiled. He stepped up next to Nini. He didn't touch her, but moved in a way that implied warmth and even love. I looked at them together and smiled. Maybe she was right.

"Hey Logan. Nice to see you. It's been a while."

"Yeah! You still skating, or just tearing it up on the bike?" Logan asked.

"Once in a while. You?"

"I go down to Venice sometimes, skate the boardwalk. You gotta come down and check it out. There's some sick kids down there." He looked at Nini while he said this, and

I understood he was asking her to come.

"Sounds rad," I said.

I rode alone. Franny rode with Bart, and Logan sat behind Nini. It was an odd shape they made, a tiny woman riding a full-size man on her big bike. But he seemed to enjoy it. He kept his arms wrapped around her waist and his chin nuzzled into her shoulder.

Bart kept the pace and was in a particularly fast mood. Nini and I traded for second. We took Marshall-Petaluma Road out of town and hooked a left onto Hwy 1. Bart took the first hairpin too fast and slid into the gravel. His back tire broke free, and he and Franny tipped over the embankment and disappeared. Nini and I quickly pulled over, and the three of us ran back to the curve where they'd disappeared. There, lying about 10 feet below us, in a softly padded patch of marsh grass, were Bart and Franny, laughing their heads off.

"Are you guys OK?" I yelled.

They nodded through the laughs.

"That's the luckiest spill I've ever seen," Logan said.

I slid down the embankment to help push the bike up.

Nini was quiet. Logan was the first to notice. He looked at her, but she just looked at Franny, then at Bart and me as we began to push the bike up.

Franny finally noticed Nini's dour face.

"What's up? We're fine." She let out one last chuckle.

"That's the curve David died on. That's where I found him."

We were all quiet. Bart and Logan hadn't known David, but they quickly got the gravity of what she was saying.

"I'm sorry for laughing," Franny finally said. "I didn't realize."

"No, I'm glad you're laughing. I'm glad you're OK. It just seems so weird that last time I was standing here, David was there. On the same ground. And he was alive, and then he was dead."

Bart kicked his bike over. It started right up. Franny climbed on, and we continued on, this time Nini setting the pace. She set it slow, and we all abided by it.

We pulled into Point Reyes to find Charles' bike parked in front of the bakery. As we parked, Charles stepped out of the café with a girl about my age. She had short hair and a boyish face. She and Charles were laughing about something. He spotted Nini, and they walked over.

"Hey Nini," Charles said.

"Hey!" Nini said cheerfully. "I was hoping we might run into you."

"Where you guys riding to?" he asked.

"Drakes probably, just out for a fun run."

"Cool. Mind if we tag along?"

"Sure! We're gonna grab a coffee, and then we'll head out. Hey Georgia," Nini said, turning her attention to the girl.

"Hey, Nini. Where you been? Haven't seen you in a while," Georgia said. I wondered how I had not met this girl, who was my age, and how or why Nini had kept her from me.

"Just around. School. I love your new haircut."

Georgia smiled. She looked at me for a brief moment, just long enough to get my gears turning.

We drank coffee and smoked, talked about Bart's accident, how lucky he and Franny were to escape unscathed. As we talked, I exchanged glances with Georgia. It was unclear whether she was "with" Charles or just hanging out. They were friendly, but didn't touch.

We mounted up and set out. Georgia rode with Charles. We wound our way out to Drakes Beach. The café was closed, so we sat on the beach for a while and smoked.

"Can I have a drag?" Georgia asked me. Charles noticed

but didn't seem to mind. I handed her my cigarette, and she took a pull on it. She looked at me through squinted eyes as she inhaled.

"I remember you. I met you once in Point Reyes. When I was like 10 or 11," she said, then handed me back the smoke. I didn't recall ever meeting her, though I wished I had, as my crush was growing by the minute. She had a very relaxed, free way about her. She laughed easily like Franny, and had an infectious way of speaking that drew you in, no matter the topic.

"I don't remember," I said, knowing that playing it a little distant usually won the day.

"Nini never even told me she had a brother."

"Nini? You never told Georgia you had a brother?" I said with a scowl.

"I figured you two knew each other. Who doesn't know anybody out here?" Nini shouted back. She and the others had drifted a little further down the beach, building something out of driftwood. It struck me as strange that she knew this girl, and I didn't. She told me everything. Or at least I had always imagined it was everything, but here it was not. I remembered her list of men. How much had she hidden from me, and why? Was she protecting me? Protecting herself? Just forgetful? Maybe I was overthinking it.

"You and Charles hang out a lot?" I asked. She could tell I was fishing and took her time responding.

"I don't know," she said, answering the question I was really asking. She turned to me, and we looked at each other for a long moment.

"What about you?"

"No," I replied.

She looked me over, and a little smile came over her face. She took the cigarette from my hand and took a drag. We walked over to the others.

"What are you guys building?" Georgia asked.

"A fire," Bart said.

"Great, I'm freezing," Georgia said with a laugh. I didn't understand why she laughed.

Charles put his jacket over Georgia's shoulders, and she smiled warmly at him. Huh, I thought, I guess it's still up in the air. I had begun to think I had made inroads, and maybe I had, but she was still clearly undecided.

Bart and Logan got the pile of driftwood burning, and we all dug in and warmed up. Georgia sat across from me, which at first seemed like a bad sign, but then I realized that she had chosen it so that we could look at each other. Which is what we did, even when Charles slid in behind her and put both his legs around her. She leaned back into his chest, but still looked at me across the fire. I didn't like this new setup, so turned my attention to Nini and Logan. They were in the same position, Logan sitting up behind Nini, with her leaning against him, her arms on his legs. She looked happy. The fire danced in her eyes, and a perpetual grin, just a slight grin, lived on her face. Logan looked happy, too. Beside me sat Bart, a cigarette dangling from his lips, and beside him sat Franny, playing with the sand. We were all quiet, watching and listening to the fire. I glanced back to Georgia. She now had her arms on Charles' legs, like Nini, her hands capping his bent knees. Well, that was it. She had decided. She didn't look at me again. Had I helped her decide by turning away? Perhaps. I thought of Nora for the first time since meeting Georgia. I stared into the fire, seeing only her glowing face, the sun beaming through her ringlets.

The ride home was cold. Charles and Georgia split off at Inverness, where Georgia gave me a half-hearted wave. I took the lead and rode fast all the way home, Nora's backlit face peering out at me from the reflections of my headlight in the thin wisps of fog we sped through.

When we arrived at home, Franny followed us into our house, leaving Nini and Logan to have the back apartment to themselves. I watched them walk away, his arm gently guiding her in the dark. He's a good guy, I thought. Even at her house, he guides her through the dark. Not forcefully, just courteously. Just as they rounded the corner, he looked back at me and smiled.

I had had a feeling Bart would get lucky, as on the way home I noticed Franny holding him extra tight, her head buried between his shoulder blades. Not watching, just trusting and holding on. Sure enough, Franny and Bart disappeared, and I sat on the couch and had one last smoke. I closed my eyes and let Nora come, drifting through my mind. I studied her face. Why wouldn't she let me go? Of course it was I who couldn't let go. I pondered this. Why? Why couldn't I let go? I didn't know. She was in me, and I couldn't get her out.

The next morning Nini came over, alone. She was quiet as she made herself a cup of coffee in the kitchen.

"How come you never told me about Georgia?" I asked. "I was like five minutes too late, and Mr. Too Much swooped in."

"I totally thought you knew each other. I swear."

I didn't know if I believed her.

"I saw your list."

She didn't respond.

"The list of guys."

"I know what list you mean."

"There's lots of things you haven't told me," I said, trying to sound nonchalant, but failing.

"So?"

"I just thought you told me everything."

"Do you tell me everything?"

"Yes."

She was quiet for a moment. I searched my mind … did I tell her everything? I did. I couldn't recall anything I found important that I hadn't described to her.

"Well, there are some things I don't tell you."

"Why?"

She searched for an answer.

"What, you only tell me the bad stuff? The good stuff? The juicy stuff? The boring stuff?" I pressed.

"I only tell you the stuff that concerns you."

Good answer. I had no comeback. I thought about the names on the list that I didn't know. Was she ashamed of them? Had they hurt her? Had she hurt them?

"But Georgia, I just really thought you guys knew each other. What's the big deal, anyway? She's with Charles."

"But she wasn't until last night. If I had known she was there …"

"Sorry."

"It's OK. So how come you keep a list, anyway?" I asked, embarrassed that I had shown cards I shouldn't have even been holding.

"So I don't forget," she said, matter-of-fact. There were a lot of names on the list. I could see how she could forget. I wondered if perhaps it wasn't better to forget some of them.

Bart and Franny came down the stairs.

"Walk of shame," Nini said.

"Yep!" Franny said, and laughed.

Nini handed her a cup of coffee as Bart lit a smoke.

"Logan asleep?" Franny asked.

"No, he left early."

We were all quiet, assuming the worst.

"He had to catch a plane to L.A. He has to work tonight."

I waited for more …

"I'm going on Friday."

"To L.A?" I asked, surprised.

"Yeah. He's buying me a ticket."

"Yay!" said Franny, clinking their coffee mugs.

On Friday Franny drove Nini to the San Francisco airport. She had been giddy with anticipation all week, and by Friday morning she was glowing with excitement. I had loaned her my camera so we could all get a glimpse of Logan's far-off world.

That weekend I wondered how she was doing, the little girl from Tomales, in Los Angeles for the first time. Would she like it? Would she meet someone famous? Would she embarrass herself? Would she still be deeply in love? Would Logan? Would she get hurt? Would he break her heart? Would he break her heart? Would he break her heart?

"We went to a party, and he introduced me to some of his friends. Mostly we hung out on the roof of his building," Nini said, as she unpacked on Monday morning. Franny and Bart were both at work, and I was happy to have Nini alone. I looked through the photos she had taken with my camera and developed first thing when she got home at the one-hour place down the hill from the house. She was eager to show me where she had been.

"You can see the whole city from up there," she said, pointing to a photo of her on the roof of a building, washed-out Hollywood all around her. She was leaning back on a sun chair, her eyes closed, with a gentle smile on her face.

"Is his house cool?"

"Yeah, it's just a small apartment in Hollywood," she said, as if she'd seen a hundred.

"Was it weird? Hollywood?"

"At first. We saw them shooting a movie on the drive home from the airport. But I got used to it. Just like anywhere else."

"Were his friends cool?"

"Yeah. Everyone was really nice."

"And what about Logan? Was he cool?"

Nini stopped unpacking and looked at me.

"He told me he loves me. He wants to take me to his mom's hotel to meet her. They're having a party next weekend, and he's going to fly up and rent a car and we'll go up."

"His mom owns a hotel?" I said, incredulous.

"Yeah, in Mendocino."

"What did you say?"

"I love him. I told him. I knew I loved him from the moment he came into work."

"Wow. That's amazing."

I noticed a Leslie Gore record that belonged to me sitting by the little record player by her bed. I picked it up.

"I love that record," she said. "You know what's funny? Logan had the same record. Can I have it?"

I looked at the cover. Leslie smiled out at me.

"I'll make you a tape. I like this record."

"Jerk."

"I said I'd make you a tape."

"Fine."

That week Nini had finals at school. I didn't see her much except late at night. On Friday I got home around seven from my new job laying carpet. Franny and Bart were sitting in the living room playing cards, drinking beer and listening to the Leslie Gore record, which I had left on the turntable.

"Where's Nini?" I asked.

"Logan picked her up. They drove up to Mendocino," Bart said as he opened another beer and set it out for me. I picked it up and took a swig.

"Oh, I thought they were leaving Saturday."

"He got off work early," Franny said.

"Ahh, well, what do you guys feel like doing tonight?"

Bart and Franny smiled at each other.

"I invited a few people over," Bart said guiltily.

"Oh, cool. Guess I'll take a shower."

I took a shower and got dressed. When I came back downstairs there were already 10 people in the house. Beer was brought in. By nine o'clock there were 35 or 40 people there.

I came out of the bathroom to find a cute young punk-rock girl who I thought I recognized.

"Hey — I know you. Don't I know you?"

"I don't think so," she said as she tried to squeeze past me.

"I think you went out with my sister's ex-boyfriend's little brother. But after my sister and he broke up. What's your name?

She smiled with a punky scowl as she shut the door in my face.

"Aura."

Later, after the party had thinned out, I noticed she was still lingering, talking to this person or that until they split, then finding someone else to talk to. It finally got down to me, Bart, Franny, Aura and Sidney, who was making out with a girl I didn't know in the kitchen. Aura was cute. She had cropped, spiky black hair and wore all black with big spiky boots.

We bullshitted for a little while, then Franny went back to her apartment. It was unclear whether Bart had been welcome to follow her or not.

"She totally wanted you to follow her," Aura said to Bart, to my surprise.

Bart smiled.

"I couldn't tell," he said.

"I think she's right," I added, sure now that Aura intended to stay.

"She usually gives me a pretty clear signal … but I guess it can't hurt to try."

Bart got up and walked through the kitchen, past Sidney and the girl, and disappeared.

Aura and I looked at each other. She smiled shyly. She didn't seem shy, but the moment was a little awkward.

"So what do you want to do?" she asked.

"I don't know. Are you staying the night?"

"I thought I might."

We went up to my room, leaving Sidney and the girl. We sat on the bed.

"My sister told me this story once about a guy who told her she couldn't sit on his bed, because if she did he couldn't resist having sex with her."

She started cracking up.

"Oh my god …"

"I know it's stupid."

"Was it Santo?"

"Oh, shit."

"Yeah."

We both laughed.

"You know him too, huh?

"Yep."

We kissed. She had small but plump lips with deep red lipstick on them. She slid her tongue into my mouth. I forced it back out and sucked on her bottom lip. She got it. She unbuckled my pants. I pulled her pants down and we laid down on the bed.

We dry humped for a few minutes as we took the rest of our clothes off.

"Are you OK?" I asked.

"Do you have a condom?" she replied. I got a condom

from under the mattress and put it on. We started fucking, but it wasn't working, the timing was off. I pulled her over on top of me. She started gyrating, but it was still off. I put my hands on her ass and pulled her to me in rhythm. She started to get it. She smiled down at me.

"Is that better?"

"Much."

She took my cues, and soon it was working quite well. I was surprised how well our bodies worked together. She reminded me of Monica, with her slender body and small breasts, but she was much more aggressive and strong. The role reversal was not lost on me.

In the morning I made her coffee, and we sat on the couch. She could make me laugh easily. But I still thought of Nora. She didn't have the power to turn that off. But still … I liked her.

"What are you doing today?" she asked.

"Nothing."

"Want to hang out with me?"

"Yeah. I do."

We walked downtown and went thrift shopping. She bought a leather tie and joked that she would tie me up with it when we got back. We ate burritos and then walked home. As we came up the driveway I noticed an unfamiliar car in the drive. Two people were standing on the porch, waiting. As we got closer I could see that it was Billie and his mother Dianne, neither of whom I'd seen in quite a while.

"Hey Billie. Hi Dianne! It's been a while." As we climbed the first step I noticed Billie's eyes were filled with tears. I looked at Dianne. Her face was a stone. She looked away.

"What's up, man? Something wrong?" I asked, wondering if it had something to do with Monica, who had long ago taken her revenge on me by sleeping with Billie, which led to a long on-again, off-again affair between the two, which sometimes overlapped precariously with my run-ins with Monica. It had been a painful trip to lose Monica over and over again to such a hero of my adolescence, but it occurred to me that he lost her over and over again to me as well, so I was at peace with it by this time, and I was happy to see him.

"It's Nini," Billie said, as the tears left his eyes and rolled down his cheeks.

"She's …" He couldn't finish.

I had no idea what he was talking about.

"She's what?"

He took a deep breath and held his hands in fists. His shoulders rose, and he looked like he was in horrible pain.

"She's dead," he finally blurted out. His body deflated.

"Huh?" I said, not registering what he meant.

"Her and Logan."

"Her and Logan what?"

"Her and Logan. They're dead. They both died."

Tears were now streaming down his face, which was bright red.

"They died?" I said, still not understanding the words.

"Nini's dead."

"What?" I said, still trying to understand.

A black hand began creeping up my back.

"They fell. Off a cliff. Somebody found them this morning in the water, on the beach."

The black hand crept over my shoulder and up my neck, gripping the back of my head.

"Nini is … dead?"

Billie just nodded. The black hand crept over my head and down my forehead. It covered my eyes. I stumbled into the house, hands out, blind. I fell to the sofa and let loose a horrendous moan. Tears gushed from my eyes. I lay there for an hour, moaning hysterically.

When I lifted my head, Bart, Franny and Aura sat around me, all with tears in their eyes. I knew it was true. I put my head back down and buried my face in the sofa.

That evening, as news spread, people gathered at our house. My mother, stepfather, younger sister, our father, our friends. We all talked and drank and smoked. Feeling ignored, Aura turned the turntable on and the Leslie Gore record came to life. "Judy's Turn to Cry" came blasting out before it got turned down to a reasonable level.

"No. Turn that off," I yelled. She turned it off, then scurried into the other room. I picked up the record jacket and looked at Leslie. She smiled at me. I shoved it into the cabinet between some other records, a horrible sense of guilt turning my stomach. Why hadn't I let Nini have the fucking record? How had Billie known about Nini and Logan? My mind raced through a series of questions it couldn't answer.

At around six o'clock a contingent of kids from Point Reyes showed up, including Georgia. Seeing her step in and look at me was the first time I could catch my breath since I had heard the news. After a few minutes of chatting with the others, I took her outside and we shared a smoke. Aura came to the door and looked out at us. I looked at her for a moment, then shook my head. I looked away. When I looked again she was gone. I needed someone who knew Nini. I just didn't need anyone else. I guess Aura understood, because I didn't see her again.

"Will you stay with me?" I asked Georgia.

"Yes. I'll stay."

That night Georgia and I lay together in my bed. We held each other and eventually we kissed. It was a strange kiss. Somehow nonsexual and completely sexual at the same time. My mind was scattered in a thousand directions, but when we kissed I felt a calm come over me. Her skin was soft and warm, and she gave it without hesitation. We spent much of the night holding each other and kissing.

The next morning the rest of my family drove up to the morgue to examine Nini's body. I did not want her dead body to be the last image I had of her, so I stayed behind. Georgia had to go home, but promised to come meet me at the hastily arranged memorial that would be held in the field beside my mother's house the next day. I spent the rest of the day sitting around the house with Bart and Franny and others that came and went, trying to keep calm. When my little sister and mother returned, I asked them if it really was Nini. Were they sure?

Yes. It was Nini. She and Logan had left the party at his mother's hotel after midnight to walk back to his cabin. They had not been seen again until they were discovered by a jogger on the beach, floating in the surf.

That night I lay in my bed, alone. I tried to picture Nini in my head. I tried to take a mental note of everything I knew about her, everything about the way she looked, the way she talked, ate, laughed. I knew it would begin to disintegrate, to slowly disappear from my memory, and she would be gone, lost to time forever, just a fading portrait. I scoured my mind for bits of information to hold onto. I could already feel the loss occurring. I tried to picture her ears and could not picture her lobes. Were they connected? What did her hands look like? How long were her fingers? I could see them still, but not her elbows. I had never looked closely enough at her elbows and now would never get the chance. Now I would never be able to look, to see her fully. Soon it would all be gone. My memories of her would be based on other memories, or photos. Did I remember her smile like that? Or did I only remember seeing a photo of her smiling like that? I tried to summon the sound of her voice, but it had already become elusive. Was it so high? No, it had more density to it. I couldn't play it back. I couldn't hear it. I panicked and sat up, lighting a cigarette. I smoked half of it and put my head back down.

I tried to sleep, but it wouldn't come. In every corner of my mind I could find only misery. I scoured my mind for a trace of meaning. "Only the good die young," I thought, then dismissed that as bullshit people tell themselves to feel better. "Everything happens for a reason." "She's in a better place." I didn't believe any of it. Why her? Why me? What if it was a mistake? What if she was really alive, and it was just someone who looked like her? No, they had gone and seen her, they were sure it was her. More bullshit. But WHY?

I went downstairs and got a beer out of the fridge. I walked into the living room to find Bart sitting on the couch, alone. His eyes were red with tears. I sat down next to him, and we shared a cigarette in silence.

HER MEN.

My mother had set up a kind of tent-like structure at the bottom of the slope of the field beside our house, and she and the rest of the family gathered there to speak. I decided I would not speak. I didn't think I could get through it, and anyway my thoughts were still so scattered I knew I would be incoherent. I had nothing to say. I sat on the ground beside the tent with Georgia and looked out at the two or three hundred people who were gathered on the hill, looking down as my mother spoke, then my father, our friends. They all described Nini — how empathetic she was, what a beautiful person she was. It was all true. And none of it helped.

I looked out at all the men. They were all there. Evan, Bodi, Marcus, Jack, Sidney, Blake, Santo, Dale, Billie, Bart … and more. I looked at Bodi's half-frozen mouth, his eyes, red and in shock. I wondered if he felt remorse for the way he had treated her. Had he ever given her any love? Or only taken it from her? Did he know she had loved him? Did he care? Did her death change anything for him?

I looked at Bart's curved face, locked in open-mouthed disbelief. I knew his impulse to protect Nini was now like a knife in his spine, twisting. Would that pain fade? How long would it take?

Sidney stared at me, then my little sister. I could see that he could still not comprehend what was happening. I looked at the many faces of men I did not know. Which of them were on the list? Which of these men with tears in their eyes and lead in their hearts had we shared her with? Which of them had loved her? They had all loved her. And I had loved her. We were all hers. And we would remain so, forever loving the fading traces of her.

I cried uncontrollably.

After the memorial service, I drove Georgia home in my younger sister's convertible, down the bay road. It was a warm, sunny day and we drove slowly, in silence. She held my hand and looked over at me, a warm smile occasionally gracing her face.

When we approached her house she took her hand from mine.

"Let's drive out to Drakes Beach," she said.

I eagerly agreed. I knew being alone with only my thoughts would be painful, and I was glad to put it off.

We parked the car in the parking lot and walked up the hill to a field, overlooking the bay, that was filled with wildflowers. I could sense something was coming. She was looking out at the horizon, not at me. Dread filled my body. The black hand rested on my shoulder.

"I've decided to stay with Charles," she said, and took my hand a final time. "I can't be with you."

I was silent.

"I'm sorry," she said.

The black hand tightened around my neck. I fought for breath. I nodded.

The drive back to her house was cold and silent. The sun had gone behind Mount Vision, and it was getting dark. I dropped her off without a word, only a short hug. I saw in my rearview mirror her watch me for a moment, then run inside. The black hand covered my mouth. I fought again for breath.

Finally alone, really alone, I wondered what it meant. To my life. Would I search for meaning in this? Would I accept it for what it was? Would I be able to choose? Or would the choice be made for me?

Lost in thought, I missed the turnoff and ended up in Olema before I realized where I was. I turned the car and headed up Hwy 1 towards Point Reyes. I passed the straightaway where Troy had bought it in Bodi's car. I thought of Troy's family. Had they found meaning in his death?

I sped up the bay road. I wished I had ridden my bike instead of driving a car. At least then I could take it out on the road, exhaust myself in a battle for each curve, grinding my pegs into the asphalt.

I passed the hairpin where Bart and Franny had run off the road and where Nini had found David, dying in the ditch. What did it mean? Did it mean anything? The place where it happened … did it have meaning? Did the cliff that killed Nini and Logan mean anything? To me? To anyone? Did the rocks below? The sea that brought them to the beach? The sand their bodies rested on? The person who found them? Did it matter who it was? Would I need to meet them? Would I need to go to the cliff, look down? What meaning would there be as I continued through life, leaving Nini farther and farther behind?

I tried to muster some anger, some rage at the world, for taking her. But I only felt sorrow. My mind was racked with division. Was there meaning in Nini's death that I would search for? That I should search for? Or was I just to accept it, live with it for what it was? How would I get through this without knowing its meaning? I knew I would never be the same again. But who would I be? Would I spend my life searching for an answer?

I pulled over and got out of the car. I looked out over the bay. The Inverness side was only silhouette now, against a pale yellow sky. I imagined Nini standing on the other side, looking back at me. What would she want? Had she known meaning in her life? She had found love, and it had found her. But did it matter? It was gone now. Nini and Logan had found love and taken it with them. It was sealed forever. But could I accept that? Accept that she was gone and that all I had left were the quickly evaporating memories of her? Would searching for a meaning in that fill this void? Or expand it? Would she approve of me just accepting it, not raging against it? And what of raging against it? There was nothing to rage against. I would be raging against myself. She was gone. I could accept it or dwell in it. I stared out into the darkness, trying to imagine her face looking back at me across the water. But all I could see was her silhouette, standing on the beach, the tiny waves lapping at her feet. Her death meant nothing more than my best friend and sister being taken from me. That was all. Nothing would change that, make it more, or less. Nothing would give her death meaning. No more meaning than her life had before she died. I knew in that moment that I had made up my mind. I took a deep breath and decided. I knew how I would live. I would accept her death, her absence. The accident that took her. I wouldn't question it. I would never ask myself "What if?" or "Why?" again. It was, and that was all. I would think of her, standing on the other side, in the darkness, looking back at me … waiting for me.

I drove on, alone.